HER OWN SPECIAL ISLAND

Santa Maria was home to Linda Ransom. She had been born there, and had spent a happy childhood on the lush, sun-baked Caribbean island. The one thing she wanted more than anything else was to return . . . When the opportunity came of a position as governess on the island she was overjoyed — full of anticipation for her new life. But somehow things began to go wrong . . . her ten-year-old pupil proved to be a spoilt, undisciplined child . . . the friends she remembered from the past seemed to be distant and afraid . . . and the island itself had changed . . . Santa Maria that had been such a happy place was now sinister and dangerous . . . dangerous even to Linda Ransom . . .

Books by Nora Lofts in the
Ulverscroft Large Print Series:

JASSY
THE BRITTLE GLASS
A CALF FOR VENUS
QUEEN IN WAITING
MADSELIN
HEAVEN IN YOUR HAND
SCENT OF CLOVES
LOVERS ALL UNTRUE
HER OWN SPECIAL ISLAND

———————◆———————

This Large Print Edition
is published by kind permission of
TRANSWORLD PUBLISHERS LTD.
London

NORAH LOFTS

HER OWN SPECIAL ISLAND

Complete and Unabridged

ULVERSCROFT
Leicester

First published in Great Britain in 1973
Previously published in the U.S.A. under
the title *Uneasy Paradise*

First Large Print Edition
published July 1975
SBN 85456 354 7 ✓

This special large print edition is
made and printed in England for
F. A. Thorpe, Glenfield, Leicestershire

1

MRS. GORDON said, "My husband is a practicing optimist." She flicked the ash from her cigarette and the heavily laden charm bracelet on her thin wrist jangled. "To be honest, I thought his advertizement was a complete waste of effort. I thought governesses were as extinct as the dodo. And it isn't as though Santa Maria were a well-known place to which a young woman would wish to go, by whatever means. I did not know of its existence until my husband accepted this post there. Miss Ransom, why did you answer the advertizement?"

"Because I was born there. I have always wanted to go back. Always. But until this moment — No, I must not take too much for granted, must I? Until I saw Mr. Gordon's advertizement, I thought I had missed my chance forever," Linda said.

"Tell me about it."

"Well, I was born there and it was such

a happy place. And there was a school, a convent school. It provided a good education up to a point but it was not designed to fit girls to earn a living. My father was a doctor; he saw that he could not give great parties, or provide me with a dowry . . . Mrs. Gordon, that may sound to you a very archaic term, but when I was young, on Santa Maria dowries still mattered. So I was sent to England, to Felixstowe to be educated for a career."

"As a teacher?"

"No. My father hoped that I should become a doctor. But that was impossible."

Shut away, do not even remember now those failures, fainting away when a bullock's heart was dissected and inside her own rib cage she felt, idiotically, the knife. Miss Smith saying, "I am afraid, Linda, that you have not the necessary detachment. . . ."

"So I decided to teach, instead. I always thought that once qualified, I could go back to Santa Maria. As a teacher."

"But you did not?" Mrs. Gordon had a light, pleasant voice. She conducted an inquisition as though it were a conversation.

"No," Linda said. "For three reasons. There was an outbreak of typhoid; both my parents died. Then my aunt, my father's sister who had been unbelievably kind to me, having me for holidays . . . she developed the most crippling arthritis, quite suddenly. As soon as I was qualified — that is six years ago — I took a post in a school near to where she lived, and looked after her as well as I could. . . ."

Shut that away, too; shopping, cleaning, every day beginning with the care of a woman grown querulous from pain and helplessness; every evening washing clothes, cooking food, washing dishes . . . catching the bus.

"She died in June. But in the meantime the president had passed a law that all teachers must by bilingual in English and Spanish."

"I see," Mrs. Gordon said. "May I give you another cup of tea?"

It was November, but the sitting room in the hotel was as warm as summer; there were carnations on one table, pink lilies, almost overpoweringly sweet-scented, on another. In the midst of the luxury Mrs. Gordon, wearing a long loose garment of pleated chiffon, reclined upon a sofa, looking very precious and rather frail. The idol at the heart of the shrine. She was quite fair and her eyes were the color of a Siamese cat's.

"You are aware of the changes on the island?" The casual question had hidden purpose.

"Oh yes. You know how it is, when one is interested in a place or a person the name seems to leap out. Actually, since Independence, Santa Maria had not been much in the news."

"I expect you have retained contact. Friends? Relatives?"

Linda's expression changed.

"I had two friends at school and we corresponded regularly for some time, but it is years now since I heard. Relatives? None."

So the suspicion that the young woman had applied for the job in order to get her fare paid seemed to be unfounded. Mrs. Gordon would have liked to ask — What about the men in your life? But she thought better of it.

"I'll speak frankly," she said. "I think that if you take the post and come with us, you should promise to stay with us for at least a year. Would you be willing to do that ?"

"Before I committed myself I should like to see Sarah."

"How very sensible. But at the moment she is with her grandmother in Paris. My husband is in Hanover, inspecting some machinery. He will collect her and they will join the ship at Cherbourg. It is rather a pity that you left answering the advertizement until so late."

"It was by pure chance that I saw it at all. I don't take that paper. I happened upon it, wrapped round a root of celery."

"In any case, seeing Sarah, even spending a day with her, would tell you nothing, Miss Ransom. She is very . . . well, variable is the word, I suppose. My husband's work has taken him abroad a good deal and whenever the climate and other circumstances have been suitable we have had her with us. At other times she has stayed with her grandmother in Paris, or her other grandparents in Scotland, and she has been thoroughly spoiled. She has had no proper education and is at once extremely precocious and abysmally ignorant. I can show you a photograph of her — not that that will mean anything, either."

The bracelet jangled as she dived into a crocodile handbag and took out a folder of the same material. Opening it and handing it over she said, "She is not a nitwit."

Linda found herself looking at the most beautiful and vibrantly intelligent face she had ever seen on a child.

She said, without thinking, "She reminds me of a portrait . . . Emma Hamilton when young; that rather rare crayon drawing . . ."

About Emma who became Lady Hamilton and Nelson's mistress opinion was sharply divided, but few mothers, however pro-Emma they were, would welcome the comparison. It was one of those things that should be thought, but not said. However, Mrs. Gordon laughed.

"Do you know, I have often thought so. I once said it and George, that is, my husband, was profoundly shocked. But the likeness is there, not in face only. I haven't the slightest doubt that if Sarah were thrown into the world tomorrow — as Emma was, with nothing but her looks and her wits — she would survive and make some impact. Not in the same way, of course. The courtezan, like the governess, is a thing of the past. And that seems to have brought us full circle, does it not?"

Somehow that was not the speech of a stupid woman, too idle, too much concerned with her own appearance and her social life, to undertake the care of her own daughter.

"Mrs. Gordon, may I ask you something?"

"Anything you like. If there is the slightest prospect of our living together we should get off on the right foot. Ask away. No! There is no need. I know. Why has Sarah been left to servants who spoiled her and to grandparents? Why does she need a governess? Miss Ransom, if I tell you this, and if you decide to become part of the family, you must forget what I am about to tell you, and never refer to it, even indirectly. Is that understood? Very well. When I was sixteen and at school I had rheumatic fever, in a sly kind of way, never diagnosed. It left me with a valvular lesion in my heart. Nobody knew." She gave Linda a bitter-sweet smile. "I lost my place on the hockey team. Puffing like a grampus. Then there were dances and I never could manage more than a half. It seemed so silly. Girls much fatter . . . However, I managed. And I married. It was not until I was well and truly pregnant that anyone knew what was wrong with me. Having Sarah did not improve things and George does so *blame* himself that I must make light of it. In fact, I took advantage of his absence and went to a man in Harley Street . . . Not exactly encouraging, but honest. With the minimum risk, no excitement, no exertion, two cigarettes a day and half a glass of sherry at functions. You see?"

"Yes. I am very sorry," Linda said.

"But there is no need to be. My disability is relatively mild. People are *born* blind, or deaf and dumb or crippled. And even the normal — doomed from birth; every birth certificate a death warrant. The only thing is to make this little space," she moved her thin hands and measured it off in the air, "happy for ourselves and for those who have to deal with us. Golden lads and girls all must as chimney sweepers come to dust . . . But the interim should be as pleasant as possible."

Linda closed the folder and handed it back.

"If you wish it, Mrs. Gordon, I will come with you and I promise to stay for a year."

"Out of pity? I disapprove of it as a motive for major decisions."

"So do I. You want a governess; I want to return to Santa Maria. Could we leave it at that?"

"Most willingly," Mrs. Gordon said. She smiled for the first time and Linda could see that she had once been very pretty, too. "I think we should all have a very happy year together."

2

SARAH, seen in the flesh and in color was even lovelier than in the photograph, but for the first forty-eight hours, as the *Columbia* steamed away, out of the slush and fog of the English winter and toward the sunshine, Linda wondered whether her pupil was going to contribute much toward that happy year. She was affronted by the idea of having a governess at all and treated Linda with polite hostility. She was ten years old, rather tall for her age and supremely self-confident, so that at times she seemed much older.

"I thought that governesses went out with *Jane Eyre*," she remarked. "In any case we shall have no lessons until we arrive; so do you mind if I call you Linda? I mean, if I go about calling you Miss Ransom and you call me Sarah it will seem a very odd relationship to people who think that governesses went out with *Jane Eyre*."

Linda had met awkward girls before,

sometimes as many as forty in one class-room. This was slightly different, but the old rule held, some kind of dominance must be established if any progress were to be made.

"Linda is my name," she said placidly. "And it has not been used lately. To be called by it will delight me, Sarah." From behind the beautiful eyes something seemed to peep, only a flicker, like an old woman twitching a curtain aside; but different, definitely a challenge. "I am a little surprised," Linda said, "that you should mind what people think."

The thing took another peep. "Oh, for myself I do not mind at all. I just thought that people might think you were Daddy's secretary. People, I mean, who have never heard of *Jane Eyre.*"

Linda said, "That book seems to have made a great impression on you."

"I absolutely love it. People make such a fuss about *Wuthering Heights*, which is quite incredible, and dull into the bargain. *Jane Eyre* is real."

"Well then," Linda said, "we have one thing in common; a preference for Charlotte Brontë."

The thing looked out and said — You don't catch me that way!

"It is a minority opinion," Sarah said.

*　　*　　*

Next day she assumed a mothering attitude. "Daddy, I think you should change places with Linda, what with you and that man who puts all his trotters in the trough, she has no view at all."

"Darling!" Mr. Gordon said. Sarah's voice carried. But he got up and said, "Miss Ransom, if you would prefer to sit here."

He was a man who without being fat gave an impression of being so, especially when he was seated. He had a wide, plump face, set in cheerful lines, a body like a barrel; a great solid lump of a man — until you looked at his hands, narrow and elegant and always on the fidget. He twirled his glass, he rearranged things on the table, he lighted his cigar with the maximum of ceremony. Far, far less stolid then he looked, Linda had decided.

At Sarah's bidding they changed places.

Sarah said, "I think it is *disgusting*. All I get asked to is the children's party. Stupid little girls turning their toes in and stupid little boys chewing their nails. And Coca-Cola! I shan't go to it. So I do think you might take me to this purser's party. Nobody would notice."

"If your parents thought you should go to cocktail parties, Sarah, they would have taken you with them last evening." Sarah muttered and scowled, lolling on Linda's bed and watching her prepare for the party with a critical eye which seemed to belittle each move.

"Your daddy," Linda said, growing restive under this supervision, "arranged to play table tennis with you. He'll be waiting."

"Table tennis is an unsuitable game for stout, elderly gentlemen."

"That is a most ungrateful thing to say!"

"Yes, isn't it? Are you going like *that*? Haven't you a wrap of any kind?" Linda's life, except for one brief period, best forgotten, had not included much frivolity. The dress she had now put on was a relic of those days.

"I shan't need a wrap; it will be warm enough."

"When you get there; I know. I've been to cocktail parties. My grandmère never excluded me from anything. But the passages are drafty. And there is another reason why you should have a wrap. Everyone else will. You'll look under-privileged." She jumped from the bed. "I'll borrow one of Mummy's. She has at least four."

"Sarah, please. I am quite all right as I am. I don't need a wrap and I don't wish to borrow." Then, as Sarah made for the door, Linda moved faster and stood with her back to it. The thing that lived behind the very blue eyes looked out, almost dangerously. Then Sarah laughed.

"And there you will stand, even if you miss the party! All right, if you wish to look like an orphan child with all that mink around, do it. It seems to me the most *peculiar* thing. I'm always being told that I am selfish and ungrateful and never give a thought for others, then when I do I am forcibly prevented."

* * *

The *Columbia* was a luxury liner, always plying on cruises; Iceland in mid-summer, the West Indies in mid-winter, the Mediterranean in spring and autumn. The purser was a man of social talent and vast experience. In the time that it took him to shake hands and exchange a stereotyped greeting, he had his guests sorted in an almost infallible file system. Age, income, class, social expertise or ineptitude. People who arrived in pairs did not demand immediate attention, they could talk to one another for a few minutes. If after the first round of drinks they were still talking to one another, he consulted his mental file and took action. Of people who arrived singly, some could safely be left alone. There were women, both old and young, who entered with an air of saying — Well, here I am, now the party can begin! There were men, both young and old, who cast a calculating glance over the assembly and made for the most attractive woman in sight. But there were others who needed a little nursing along, and to pair them off was not only a duty, a convenience, but a pleasure.

"May I introduce Mr. Hamilton? Miss Ransom. I have an idea that you are both bound for the same place." He did not name it. Let them do that; give them something to talk about whether his assumption was right or wrong. He moved away to do something for a woman, well-dressed, overjewelled, who in reply to his greeting had said, "Pleased to meet you", and then gone into a corner and there stayed. There was a couple who had used that same phrase, he picked them out with an unerring marksman's eye, introduced them, using the same little trick, and passed on. He enjoyed a deserved popularity and was remembered by a surprising number of passengers at Christmas.

"I'm going to Santa Maria," Linda said to Angus Hamilton.

"Then he was right. It's odd, I got talking yestereay to a man in the bar; he's going there too. A Mr. Gordon. We discovered that we're part of the same package deal."

"Mr. Gordon is actually my employer."

"You a sugar expert, too?"

"No; I am governess to Mr. Gordon's daughter."

The purser had been absolutely correct in his assessment of young Mr. Hamilton's social grace. Handed this piece of information, he said, "My God! I don't envy you."

"Why do you say that?"

"Well, maybe I shouldn't. But she struck me . . . I mean, there we were, having a most interesting talk and she burst in demanding sherry. He offered her everything else, up to something called Babycham, but sherry she would have. And she got it! Then, of course, he had to go with her into the lounge where bairns *are* allowed. Can you cope with her?"

"I hope to, given time." To change the subject she said, "*Bairns*. Are you Scots?"

"I am that."

They were now under way. She told him that she had been born in Santa Maria and then asked what he meant by a package deal; and he explained; he was veterinary surgeon, going out on a three-year contract to organize a new animal health service and center; part of President Fernandez' crash program for the modernization of the island economy.

Linda said, "Things do work out strangely. When I was a child José Fernandez was a young soldier and he used to visit our cook so often, and always hungry, that my father sometimes said that we could not afford to keep Manuela. You see my father was a doctor and he was very much concerned with the poor; he did a great deal of work for nothing, so he was poor himself. Now, I am sure that had he lived and seen how that hungry young soldier was to take charge and make all the reforms that he has done, he would be delighted to think that in a way he had contributed."

That, the purser thought, was a good pairing off. Mr. Hamilton, Miss Ransom were deep in conversation, looking animated and interested in one another, no eye roaming, as sometimes happened, saying, "Rescue me".

The steward who had stood by the door and announced the name of each newcomer had done his duty and gone away; people would arrive a quarter of the way through, halfway through, but no later than that. Sarah walked straight in.

* * *

Mr. Gordon had waited in the recreation room. He had insisted that Linda should go to the party and assured her that he would entertain Sarah until dinnertime. When she did not arrive, ten minutes, a quarter of an hour, twenty minutes late, he was relieved. He loathed table tennis. It was, in any case, unsuitable for a man of his weight and age; and he was wrong, win or lose. If he lost Sarah said he was not trying and if he used his good eye and flexible wrist to make a really killing stroke, she turned surly. And, even more to be considered was the fact that when he was playing with Sarah he was not looking after Juliet. He had left her in good company, playing bridge with three amiable people, a married couple and a sister-in-law, but there was danger even there. Juliet, when playing bridge, which she did expertly, was inclined to forget time, and none of those whom she played with could know how delicate she was. Only he knew that. When after twenty minutes Sarah had not turned up, he assumed gladly that she had found some more attractive occupation and made his way to the card room, where, at the first opportune moment he said, "Darling, I think that will do," and took his wife away to have that necessary rest before dinner.

The bridge-playing wife said, "Edgar, if ever you did that to me I should divorce you!" The unmarried sister-in-law said, "Thank God I never married!"

*　　*　　*

Unimpeded, Sarah joined the party. She had put up her hair so that it formed in front a fringe and at the back what was called a French knot. She had applied a good deal of cosmetics to her face, and wore a frock, bought for her by a doting grandmother in Paris, a beautiful blue, and over it a mink stole, of the gray color called slate. Over her arm she carried another, a golden cream color. At a party slightly less successful than the purser's her arrival would have made a sensation. As it was her entry was unnoticed.

"Linda, darling," she said, having pushed through the throng to where Linda and Angus Hamilton had just reached the point of exchanging Christian names, "I have brought your wrap. You left it on the bed." The impish thing was not now merely peeping, it was staring out, defiant. And the gesture with which the still childish hands flung the beautiful fir over Linda's shoulders was the equivalent of a smack in the face.

"But I told you," Linda said, the expostulation sounding feeble, "that I did not need a wrap."

A steward, making his last round, proffered a tray of glasses; the sherry was brown, the ready-mixed gin and dry martini pale. Sarah reached for the paler drink and was forestalled. Angus Hamilton put out his competent hand and took her by the wrist.

"You've had enough," he said. To the steward he said, "Thank you, no. We must be moving." Still holding Sarah's wrist in what looked like an affectionate gesture but was actually a grip of iron he made his way to the door. Linda followed. Outside the door Angus released his hold. Sarah looked at him so venomously that he half expected verbal or physical assault; but she spoke to Linda. "Miss Ransom, you really should choose your pick-ups more carefully." With great dignity she walked away.

"D'you think her parents know of this prank?" Angus asked.

"No. They are indulgent, but not to that extent."

"Will you tell them?"

"I think not. No point in worrying them."

"They should damn well be worried! Bringing up a monster like that and then handing it over for somebody else to deal with. Not that's it any affair of mine. When'll I see you again?"

"Oh," she said, deliberately vague, "we're always about somewhere."

"Don't you get any free time?"

"It's all more or less free, for the duration."

"Well, look. Let's try to have a drink before lunch tomorrow; in the Rainbow Lounge. Bring the Monster, if you must, but she'll get no sherry from me!"

* * *

"Linda has found herself a beau," Sarah said at the dinner table. "Not handsome enough. And with red hair, a sign of foul temper. Look, she's blushing!"

"So are you, unless . . ." Mr. Gordon replaced the spectacles which he had laid aside after studying the menu. "What have you done to yourself. What's happened to your hair? Is that *rouge*?"

"I found myself in such a difficult position," Sarah said airily. "Linda really needed a wrap and I went to borrow one of Mummy's; but by that time Linda had gone. And I knew that they wouldn't let me in if I looked my age. So I did my face like this, and my hair. And I got in easily. I was even offered sherry. I didn't drink it, though," she added self-righteously.

Mr. Gordon, who had rescued his wife and suggested that she should dine in her cabin, seemed to see nothing extraordinary about this tale. What he noted was that Linda lacked a wrap and being an extremely generous man, and already grateful to Linda for keeping Sarah occupied for so many hours of what might have been tedious days, he began to wonder whether the ship's shop had something decorative. Sure to have.

Linda sat and thought — how clever! Getting her word in first, in case I said something. And the cleverest part about it was that it was true. A tale told from a particular angle; a few words omitted; but not a lie anywhere. In fact, Sarah was clever enough to see that lies were the refuge of the stupid.

"Well," Mr. Gordon said, "I don't want you growing up before your time. Youth's a time will not endure. You should make the most of it." He removed his glasses, the better to see at a distance. "Peaches," he exclaimed. "Sarah, don't you think it would be nice if you went along and took Mummy a couple? She'd rather see you than a stewardess."

"And while I'm gone," Sarah said, "Linda can tell you about her beau."

★　　★　　★

"I did get into conversation with a young man with red hair," Mr. Gordon said. "Very sound fellow, I thought. Veterinary. Going to Santa Maria. Is that the one?"

"Yes. Sarah exaggerates, of course. We were introduced and found that we were both going to Santa Maria. And he spoke of you. That was all."

"He'll be in Port Philip most of the time," Mr. Gordon said musingly. "Less than twenty miles from Caterina. We must ask him out as soon as we're settled. Other people, too, of course. That is something I've wanted to speak to you about, Miss Ransom. In many ways Sarah is a bit backward. Never had a chance. But she is sharp as a needle. I don't think you'll have any bother over the lessons, and in any case I don't think a ten-year-old should be too much tied down. So if you could and would help my wife with the *social* side of things . . . I'm going to be as busy as a one-armed paperhanger, I can see that. And she . . . she isn't very strong. Anything you can take on yourself, I should be most extremely grateful."

Could you possibly say — I'm not strong enough to deal with Sarah. Return the fare money. Find another job. The answer was that you could not. The element of trust and confidence in that little speech was completely disarming. And both the parents were so nice; kind, considerate, easygoing. Linda would very gladly have taken on the job of housekeeper-cum-social secretary to Mrs. Gordon, or office secretary to Mr. Gordon. It was Sarah whom she . . . disliked? No, one could not dislike a child of ten. Feared? That sounded even more impossible. Was disconcerted by? That was nearer the mark.

She said, "I had realized that Mrs. Gordon was not very robust. And she may at first find the climate trying. I'm one of the native born, I shall be in my element. And I'll do to and see to everything I possibly can."

"Good girl," he said, smiling at her. "I knew you were a good girl the moment I set eyes on you." His hands began to fidget. "I was very careful about the climate, to ask about it, before making my decision. Caterina is well above sea level. I was assured that it would not be too hot. And they promised air conditioning in the house. And plenty of domestic help . . ." That and a vastly enhanced salary was what had persuaded him to join what was called the brain-drain. In so few places nowadays could one get steady help no matter what one paid; and a man with an invalid wife — though Juliet would never admit to being that — had to think of these things.

3

"YOU girls go and sit down. I'll see to this. Shouldn't take long," Mr. Gordon said. He took the four passports and went to join a short queue at the passport control.

The man in charge wore military uniform very trim and smart, khaki with black buttons and facings.

He took his time. "Mr. Gordon?" He carefully studied the photograph and its owner, and then stamped a page.

"I am afraid, sir, that I must ask the ladies to present themselves."

"My wife is not strong. She is quite unable to stand about," Mr. Gordon said with the faint truculence that always came over him when he was protecting Juliet from someone or something.

"Which is your wife, sir?"

"The lady in blue, with the fair hair." Which one did he think, the officious fool?

"She may remain seated. Perhaps you

would ask her to remove the sunglasses."
That done he seemed to be satisfied about
Mrs. Gordon's identity. Even Sarah he did
not pass without scrutiny. Then, with
Linda's passport before him, he said,

"You were born in Santa Maria, madam.
You present yourself through that door."
He pointed and returned her passport.

It opened into a fair-sized room with a
wide window looking out upon a ware-
house. Seated at a desk, with her back to
the window was a woman, and that people
carry about with them some essential
personality was proved by the fact that at
sight of her Linda thought — Mrs. Sarmiento! It could hardly be. A strong
resemblance, perhaps even a kinship. No
woman could have changed so much or
changed so little.

Mrs. Sarmiento had kept the post office
and the tiny general shop in Nelson Bay,
the place where Linda had been born. She
had had a wealth of black hair, always so
insecurely pinned that it was on the point
of falling down. She had a full, fattish
figure, clad in dresses of bright artificial
silk, always soiled. She was a widow with
no children of her own, but she had a

sister who had eleven, some of whom were always in the shop. "Eating all the profit," Dr. Ransom had said, "and not very hygienic." Linda had been permitted to buy only wrapped sweets and forbidden absolutely to drink lemonade from the open container to which was tied a chipped enamel mug.

The woman behind the desk had hair cropped in a mannish style; she wore a shirt of khaki silk with black collar and cuffs. She did not look good-natured or harassed; in fact her squarish, olive-tinted face wore a look of almost Buddhist calm. And it was, it was Mrs. Sarmiento. The first link with the old life!

"Mrs. Sarmiento," Linda said, moving her passport to her left hand and reaching out her right. "You won't remember me, but I remember you. I'm Linda Ransom!" Then she was certain that after all she was mistaken. No answering smile, no look of recognition, no attempt to take the outstretched hand. Yet the woman said,

"Oh yes, Miss Ransom. I remember you. I have a good memory for faces." She injected into the last words a slightly sinister meaning, as though in the past

Linda had done her some injury, still resented. Yet surely any memory Mrs. Sarmiento retained should be tinged with warmth; she, her sister, her eleven nephews and nieces, had all at some time or another had free medical attention. Every article of clothing that Linda outgrew was passed on to be worn by Poppy, the niece nearest in size, and whenever Mrs. Sarmiento had trouble with her post office accounts, which, being official, must be kept correctly, she had gone crying to Dr. Ransom, who sometimes had to supply more than arithmetic in order to make them come right.

"If you will sit down," Mrs. Sarmiento said. "From time to time, people do come back and it is part of my duty to ask why."

"I came back because I always wanted to. And because I was offered a job here."

"As a schoolmistress?" Mrs. Sarmiento asked, after glancing at the passport.

"No, as governess to the daughter of a sugar technologist who has come to work at Caterina."

"One child," Mrs. Sarmiento commented. It sounded like an accusation. Linda ignored it. What had the size of Mr. Gordon's family to do with this woman, grown so unfriendly and officious? "You consider that a worthy occupation?"

"I never thought about it."

"You should. President Fernandez has worked miracles; but trained people are too few. You are trained?"

"Yes."

"Then your place is with the educational service in your native country."

"I hoped once to teach here. But I have no Spanish."

"You could take a course. Every road is now open to everyone. Consider me. At the age of thirty-eight I went to school for six months and am now a qualified civil servant."

"You are to be congratulated, Mrs. Sarmiento. I may even consider your suggestion. But not yet. I am under contract to Mr. Gordon for a year." She was glad to be able to say that. The course proposed by Mrs. Sarmiento, a course perhaps similar to the one which had so dehumanized her, did not seem very attractive. "Mr. Gordon and his family are waiting for me now," she added.

"Of course." Mrs. Sarmiento gave the passport a sharp blow.

Outside, the luggage had been loaded and Mrs. Gordon and Sarah had taken their seats in a large, official-looking black car. Mr. Gordon stood talking to a young man who, though introduced as Mr. Parker, showed little other sign of being English. He was, indeed, almost a typical Santa Marian. The island had had a curious history; Spanish, French, English in turn had owned it. It had always been the Cinderella of whichever national family held it; as a result it had attracted little attention, and few pioneers. It had been very difficult for all but a few families of the original Spanish settlers to preserve their blood unmixed by other strains and the situation had been confused by the period of French occupation during which there was no color bar, and by the fact that in the early nineteenth-century, when England had taken over — Nelson Bay, by its name, commemorated a victory — the English were already antislavery. All the lines of what was called the underground railway had not run north into the antislavery states of America; some had run south, and Santa Maria had received its share of true Negroes, mulattoes, octaroons and men

32

and women who, in anywhere but the Southern states could "pass for white". The result was a mixture in which the Spanish strain predominated, not only in appearance, but in religion and manners. Names gave no clue. Mr. Parker could have presented himself at the court of Philip II in Madrid and been quite unnoticed.

"I am sorry that you should have been so much delayed," he said. "And now I shall drive very slowly, if that is agreeable to you, so that you may see our capital."

It was changed. The Gordons looked upon novelty, Linda upon remembered scenes. Her visits to Port Philip had been rare and for that reason more impressive. The bones of the place had changed little. There were fewer beggars, fewer donkeys, more cars, more men in uniform. Soldiers? Police? But the center of the city, laid out long ago in a system of streets, meeting at right angles and at each intersection in a square, had not changed at all. St. Peter's Cathedral still dominated one, the governor's — now the president's — palace another. Then came the shopping center, side by side with the public gardens —

the gift of some long-dead governor's wife.

A little further out the scene changed. Glass and concrete bootboxes.

"The Technical College," Mr. Parker said. "And the hospital." At the risk of his driving he turned his head. "It was an iniquity," he said. "For your father, who had done so much and believed so much, no memorial could have been enough, and while it was being built it was always referred to as the Ransom Memorial Hospital. Indeed many people still so refer to it. But when the statues were removed, it was necessary to be consistent."

"I quite understand," Linda said. "And I know that my father would have been delighted to see such a splendid new hospital, never mind the name."

Mr. Parker continued to point out things of interest until the streets gave way to a belt of market gardens and small farms, the produce of which went into the market of Port Philip every morning.

"This," he said, disapprovingly, "is still a backward area. The holdings are too small. Much could be done by co-operation."

"I wonder it has not been tried," Mr. Gordon remarked.

"It has, in part. Not very successfully," Mr. Parker admitted. "It takes a generation for the hoe to give way to the tractor." He began to drive faster. The road ran uphill, quite steeply. All trace of cultivation, even of human habitation, was left behind; on either side of the road stood the virgin forest, mingling every shade of green.

"Do you have wolves?" Sarah asked suddenly. She had been unusually unself-assertive during the drive, leaning forward and seeming to hang upon Mr. Parker's near monologue and paying absorbed attention to everything he pointed out. Now and again she gave Linda a little nudge and followed it by a grimace indicative of disgust. Linda could not imagine why. Precocious as she was, Sarah was surely too young to share Linda's own mounting feeling that Mr. Parker, except when speaking of the hospital, sounded as if he had learned his patter a trifle too well.

"We have no dangerous animals in Santa Maria, Miss Gordon. And now we are coming to the plantation area; now all nationalized."

The countryside leveled out and although the forest continued to run beside them on the righthand side of the road, the land on the left, as far as eye could see, was under cultivation.

"Ah," Mr. Gordon said. "Sugar cane!" He spoke with satisfaction.

"Maize also," Mr. Parker said, using the strictly English word. "Now I will slow down and if you look to the left you will see the mills and beyond the town of Santa Barbara — the Workers' Paradise as it is called. The houses all new, with correct sanitation; a school and a clinic. Here we turn to the right and within a few minutes shall be in Caterina. I hope that you will think it beautiful."

It was. A small colony of houses, all different and yet all conforming; Spanish colonial style modified for twentieth-century use. Linda remembered the house in which she had spent her youth, a truly old Spanish house with the Moorish influence still strong. All the pretty features locked away in its central courtyard, a blank face turned to the world. These houses looked as though someone had taken such a house and turned it about, trying out

36

variations and yet adhering to the basic pattern; the courtyard in front, the courtyard to the side. Walls pink, shutters white; walls white, shutters hyacinth blue; walls sea-green, shutters crimson.

"That," Mr. Parker said, indicating a house with rose-pink walls and maroon trim, "is my home. And this, Mr. Gordon, is yours." It was white with olive-green shutters.

Mr. Parker brought the car to a standstill and sounded the horn. Two people who must have been watching and listening appeared. To Linda, familiar products of another dominant strain, the original islanders who had survived all — invasion and exploitation and imported disease. "You may not believe this," her father had once said over the lunch table, "but today I saw an Ameringo carrying a piano — not a grand, a cottage piano, like ours — on his back. I doubt whether a donkey could have done it. I was so interested that I followed him and when he put it down — in that dump which still pretends to be French — Relais des Fleurs or some such name — I went up and asked him if I might take his pulse and his blood pressure;

and do you know, both were absolutely normal. I wouldn't have believed it if anyone had told me. . . ."

Theresa, middle-aged, Juan, still young, but both cut out of the same fiber, tough and resilient answered the summoning horn.

"Theresa," Mr. Parker said, "will keep house and cook; will wash and iron. Juan will help her; he will serve at table; he will shop — he has a bicycle — he will wash windows, and the car, and of course look after the garden."

And if Santa Barbara could be called the Workers' Paradise, Caterina might be called the Executives' Heaven. Exactly what Mr. Gordon had wanted for his wife and failed to find elsewhere. Poor darling, she thought she had deceived him, but she had not. Carefully tended, spared any strain or stress, she might live for five years. And here with Theresa, Juan, Miss Ransom, and such care as he himself could provide, the years would be happy — and perhaps even extended.

"I will leave you," Mr. Parker said, as Theresa and Juan began to unload, handling heavy cases as though they weighed nothing. "I should be gratified, if when you have settled in, you would dine with me, Mr. and Mrs. Gordon and Miss Ransom. Not a large party, a meeting of colleagues. At nine o'clock?"

"Well, if my wife feels up to it . . ."

"Oh, I shall," Mrs. Gordon said. "By nine o'clock I shall be completely restored. Thank you, Mr. Parker."

"And what about me? Am I not invited?" Sarah asked.

Mr. Parker then said something that parents and grandparents should have said long ago.

"I am sorry. I was under the impression that children of good family went to bed before nine o'clock." It was framed as an apology, but it was not that. It appeared to leave the invitation open-ended, should either parent express a wish for the child to be included, but actually it was a challenge.

"Sarah and I will see to the unpacking," Linda said, ending the awkward moment, "and then we will both have an early night. Thank you, Mr. Parker."

"There will be other times," he said. "Until this evening then . . ." As he turned back to the car and was still well within earshot Sarah said in her carrying voice, "How awful it must be to spit when you talk!"

4

"**P**RACTICALLY it amounts to false pretences," Mr. Gordon said, moodily sipping his dry martini. Mrs. Gordon was playing bridge at the Wilsons' house — he had looked in on his way home, assured himself that she was not too tired and would like to finish the rubber and was glad to find Linda alone. Sarah, under protest, had gone to tea with the MacNamaras who had a son, Ian, a month or two her junior, but always referred to as "that little boy". Mr. Gordon really needed to unburden his mind to somebody.

"I have looked again through all the correspondence I had with the ministry of agriculture here," he said. "Hindsight is often sharpest; but I cannot find one word to hint that I was not to be in complete control — responsible to nobody but the minister. That was the whole point; I was to reorganize, modernize, improve. Why else am I here? I've nothing against Parker as a person, pleasant chap enough, but he knows as much about processing sugar as a hog does of grand opera." He took another sip. "And that wouldn't matter if he wasn't such an interfering bastard — excuse my language. 'It is necessary, Mr. Gordon, to keep me informed,' he said, when I'd done something, technical stuff, you wouldn't understand — but then nor would he. I was on the job, I made the decision and that is what he said. Frankly, if I'd had the slightest inkling of this situation I shouldn't have come. Despite all this . . ." His glance included not only the room in which they sat, but the house, the brand-new car in the garage, the garden, the neighborhood, even Theresa and Juan — the whole Executives' Paradise. Then he recanted, "No, I shouldn't say that; it seems to suit my wife. And Sarah. And you, my dear, I hope."

They had now been settled in for a fortnight and Mr. Gordon's buoyant spirit had declined, day by day. Now she knew why. She had wondered perhaps if he had been overworking. He had worked long hours. The new machinery which he had been commissioned to buy had arrived on the specified date and he was seeing it installed. In Mrs. Gordon's presence he was able to report its arrival happily. "Very efficient, the Germans . . ." Then his face had darkened and the subject abruptly changed.

In an effort to comfort him she now said, "It seems to be the same everywhere. Angus has an overlord, too. He says he couldn't spell anatomy, let alone understand it."

"Angus. Who's he?"

"My red-headed beau. The veterinary surgeon."

"Lord, yes. Of course I remember. We must have him out here. You've seen him?"

"Yes. The evening before last. Of course you were working late. He'd heard of some place, a tourist attraction, where the seafood was wonderful, and he wanted to take me there. So I went."

"And was it? The food, I mean. Wonderful?"

"Exceptionally good. But it ended with an unpleasant incident."

"Wolf?"

"Oh no. Nothing like that. It is a very pretty place and tourists from Port Philip come round in motor boats. There's a certain amount of falsification, nonsense, you know, girls wearing very little and carrying trays on their heads. But they all loved it and the atmosphere was very pleasant. We sat about talking and watching them re-embark and decided we'd like some cold beer. It was self-service by that time, so Angus went to the bar and asked for it. There were three men drinking there — not tourists, natives, I am certain. One man said to Angus, quite normally, 'You from England?' he said he was. D'you know what the man did? He flung his tankard of beer smack in Angus' face." She paused to emphasize the drama of this.

"Angus hit him?" Mr. Gordon asked.

"He had no time. The man's friend hit him; knocked him flat in fact. And apologized very profusely. So did the barman. I did what they call mopping up operations. And then a policeman arrived; from somewhere behind the back of the bar — as though he had been *waiting*. The thing was they all looked so scared; not just the one who had been beastly. All of them. So Angus pretended it had been a head-on collision. The policeman seemed disappointed when he wouldn't complain. Myself, I'm inclined to think he was wrong. People who behave like that should be reprimanded, at least."

"He was right, you know. In fact very wise."

"Why?"

"Because the man would not have been reprimanded; or fined. He'd have had a year in jail. At least."

"For that?"

"No. For expressing what so many of them feel — an opposition to the president's policy. Incidentally the man who flung the beer must have been either very bold, or very drunk."

"He was very drunk. At least his friends said so and he pretended to be."

"I've lived in a lot of different countries in my time," Mr. Gordon said. "It gives you a kind of sixth sense and the situation here . . ."

She was never to hear what his sixth sense had told him about the situation. Mrs. Gordon and Sarah came in together in very differing moods; the mother pleased because she had won two dollars, the daughter still angry at having had to spend two hours with "that little boy".

"All we really did was entertain Rufus. I knew the Egyptians worshiped cats. The Scots worshiped dogs. I must wash my hands. After two throws a ball gets very spitty and we must have thrown it two thousand times!"

* * *

Next morning's post brought two invitations; identical except for their addresses. One for Mr. and Mrs. Gordon, one for Miss Ransom. The president desired their company at a reception to be held in the Palace. R.S.V.P.

"I shall have to have my hair done the day before," Mrs. Gordon said. Her hair was a bit of a bother; once luxurious and easy to manage, it had become tricky. From under the drier, from the skillful hands, it emerged as good as new, glistening and full-bodied. But it did not last — something to do with the pills which enabled her to go on living a seemingly normal life.

"I'll get Parker to give me a lift; then you and Miss Ransom can drive down and take your time," Mr. Gordon said with his usual obligingness. The ability to drive a car was one good thing Linda had acquired from an ill-starred love affair.

"I'll come too," Sarah said.

For once Mrs. Gordon was positive. "No, darling." She was sure now that Theresa and Juan were reliable. "You can stay here or go to Ian's." She had had experience of taking Sarah on a hairdressing expedition; in and out, "Aren't you ready *yet*?" "What are you doing *now*?" Once, in London, Sarah had said, "Then I'll go and have tea at Fortnum's and wait for you there." That relief had been dearly bought, for when Mrs. Gordon went to join her daughter, Sarah was not in the tearoom, or, so far as frenzied search could discover, anywhere in the whole vast establishment. "There was no need for panic, Mummy. I had only gone along to Hatchard's." Admittedly that was two years ago; but it had been in London where most people spoke English and the policemen were friendly. For some reason Mrs. Gordon felt that Port Philip was different. Now Sarah began to argue; Mrs. Gordon's face assumed a look of distress,

Mr. Gordon began to look worried. Linda acted, as so often, as a buffer state.

"I'll do my own hair," she said. "Then I shall be free to show Sarah something of the town."

"Well, that would solve . . ." Mrs. Gordon said. "Though actually you could do with a trim. . . ." She was, however, accustomed to accepting small sacrifices from those about her, and Linda's hair was so manageable, Linda so comparatively youthful . . .

Sarah's attitude toward Linda had now undergone a change. Nothing dramatic had brought it about and many factors had contributed to it — not least the fact that Sarah was at an age when in the ordinary way she would have been developing a "crush" on some senior schoolfellow. Added to this was the fact that Linda never cried; never told tales, did not hesitate to use the words "silly" and "tiresome", or to expose the gaps in Sarah's facilely acquired knowledge. In short, Linda did not dote upon Sarah.

On the morning of the planned trip to Port Philip Sarah was a little late for breakfast and when she did appear even

48

Linda let out a gasp half astonishment, half dismay. Sarah had taken a pair of scissors and hacked all the curls from the front and from one side of her head. Her hair, fair, but of a warmer shade than her mother's had been one of her beauties.

"My God!" Mr. Gordon exclaimed. "What have you done!"

"Fixed it so that we all have to go to the hairdresser's."

"I've a damn good mind not to let you," he said, truly angered for once. "You deserve to go about looking like a guy till it grows out again."

Sarah very seldom cried, but she had the ability to bring tears to her eyes and keep them standing there, making the blue even bluer. She did it now.

"Daddy, you would never be so cruel. I only did it because I wanted Linda to have hers done, too." Through the tears she shot a glance at Linda to see what effect this declaration of devotion and self-sacrifice might have. None! There lay the secret. Sarah actually allowed a tear to fall and spill into her orange juice.

"Are you cross, too?"

"I am appalled," Linda said coldly. "I

dread to think what will happen to you, so reckless and thoughtless and wilful."

"Has your mummy seen you?" Mr. Gordon asked, his permanent preoccupation coming uppermost. "Then she mustn't. The shock . . ." This was an emergency and he was accustomed to dealing with them. Juliet must not see Sarah until she had been tidied up a bit. His fingers beat a rapid tattoo, as his mind — not unlike Sarah's — went into action.

"Now listen to me. What time was Mummy's appointment?"

"Three o'clock."

"Then I can do it. You both go now in my car to Port Philip. Find somewhere, anywhere to do the job; if all else fails try a barber. And mind this. You've had it cut short for the sake of coolness, or to copy Miss Ransom. And not a word of this. I'll bring your mummy along and we'll all meet. Where, Miss Ransom?"

"There is a cafe, just opposite the entrance to the public gardens. It may have changed its name, but it is still there. I noticed the awnings."

"Half-past four then. Off you go!"

He had already asked Parker for the

lift; he'd be a few minutes late, irksome thought. Climbing the stairs he thought, this kind of hurry gives a man ulcers! But when he entered the bedroom — here in Santa Maria it was possible, thank God, for Juliet to breakfast in bed — his manner was calm and cheerful. He said, "Darling, we've rearranged things a bit. Miss Ransom is going to have her hair done, after all, and Sarah may have hers cut too — she finds that mop of hers rather hot here. So they've gone to squeeze in, without an appointment and I'll come and take you in myself. In that big black hearse," he said, referring in irreverent terms to the official car.

"Darling, are you sure you can spare the time? I thought this was a busy day."

"The worst will be over by two o'clock. The siesta still holds," he said.

"Then that will be lovely," she said. She smiled; she held out her thin arms under the lace and they kissed. Kisses were all he allowed himself now, but he felt no sense of deprivation; love had simply changed course. So long as she was happy and protected what else mattered? "Pick you up at about quarter past two," he said.

"You'll miss your afternoon rest, so stay in bed as long as you can."

* * *

Mr. Parker had no great wish to quarrel with Mr. Gordon; for one thing Mr. Gordon had all the know-how about all the new installations. Mr. Gordon also stood, not as parent, not as legal guardian to Miss Ransom, but in a certain capacity; a kind of primitive thing; a male in charge, suspicious of and ready to repel any invading male. Everything had changed very quickly — perhaps too quickly. But Mr. Parker was adjusting as best he could, and his attitude to Mr. Gordon was ambivalent. Mr. Gordon must be knocked down; Mr. Gordon must be placated. This seesaw relationship had been going on for a fortnight.

"It is," Mr. Parker said, referring to the big black car, "the property of the government and I am not sure that I have the power to authorize its use for an unofficial purpose, Mr. Gordon."

Sarah, bent upon getting her own way had all unknowingly sparked off something.

"Right," Mr. Gordon said, glad that the showdown come — not about something important where the relative status of works manager and general manager might be exposed in all their falsity, but over a triviality, the use of a motor vehicle for two hours and a half.

"Right," he said, happily. "I will ask permission of the minister and if he can't authorize me to use it I'll try the president. And if he's so tangled up in red tape . . . I'll hire a taxi."

"But please," Mr. Parker said, "that will not be necessary. I was only remarking that the car is for official use."

"I realize that. The very fact that I mentioned, to you, that I proposed to borrow it shows that I know what a sacred cow it is. And your uncertainty as to whether you have power to authorize me to use it shows me what a sacred sacred cow it is. I have no intention of making a habit of using it; it's just that today I'm in a bit of a fix. In fact," he said, speaking the thought aloud as it occurred to him, "I mean to buy a second car, for family use."

The car which at that moment Linda was parking in Port Philip was also, in a way, a government vehicle, since it was provided, like the house, like the furniture, like Theresa and Juan, for the use of people like Mr. Gordon. It had stood in the garage, brand new, awaiting his arrival. A good enough car but strictly utilitarian and of a make he had never encountered before, a Toledo.

"If that is indeed your intention," said Mr. Parker, rather gladly dropping the bone of contention, "I can be of help. If the order is placed, as coming from a government department, you can save twenty percent. Provided, of course, that it is a Toledo."

"I don't want a Toledo and I don't want to order through the government," Mr. Gordon said, being awkward in his turn. "I know what I want and how to get it."

"There is, of course," Mr. Parker said with a certain satisfaction, "a heavy import duty on foreign cars. I think it is now forty percent of the price in the country of origin. And they do not fare well here. At the docks — and in other places — they meet with curious accidents. And naturally spare parts always present a problem. This I say for your good."

Slightly ruffled by this conversation, Mr. Gordon turned his attention to business. But he must keep his eye on the time; Juliet was relying upon him.

*   *   *

All the most popular hairdressing establishments were busy. With the president's reception tomorrow, and every lady bidden wanting to look her best, they were working full time. There came a point when Linda thought that Mr. Gordon had been right — they must resort to a barber; but finally, in a side street, they found a place from which they emerged with almost identical coiffures, close, head-hugging caps of curls.

"You see," Sarah said, "you *do* look better. You *did* need a trim. And but for me you wouldn't have got it. Would you?"

There was only one answer. "No, I suppose not. But the whole thing was wrong. If in the first place you had agreed to stay at home, or go to tea with the MacNamaras, the question would never have arisen. Don't expect me to be grateful to you for rescuing me from a situation which you brought about."

"I had to rescue myself. It was a choice

of three. You walking about very dutiful with me. Or me left at home with Theresa and scared to death, or bored to death with Ian and his dog. I did the best I could, honestly. Linda, please; I was like the old woman and the pig that wouldn't get over the stile — you know, fire fire burn stick, stick stick beat dog, dog dog bite pig, or we shan't get home tonight. I only bit the pig, Linda."

"What do you mean by being left with Theresa and scared?"

"Oh, my usual nonsense. No, that is not quite true; she does scare me. Scared to death, is of course an exaggeration. But scared . . . I know she doesn't like me. Let's talk about something else. Lunch. I had hardly any breakfast, you know, and I am hungry."

"We can go through the gardens, I think," Linda said.

* * *

The statue of Queen Victoria had been removed; otherwise nothing had changed much; paths of pinkish gravel crossed one another at right angles between stretches of grass, kept green through the driest season. The flower beds blazed, the trees cast their shadows, the fountain splashed, just as on those days — all too rare — when Linda, on the occasional Saturday had been brought here and told the story of Lady Higham who had wished to give the place where she had been happy, some space where people could walk and sit, where children could play. Eighty years before Linda was born Lady Higham had foreseen the streets encroaching, and the market gardens, cutting people off from the countryside that was their birthright. Except by word of mouth she was not remembered. She had been one of Victoria's ladies-in-waiting and her gift to Port Philip had been given the loved name: Victoria Gardens.

Oddly enough, the rules were stricter now. Perhaps because there were more people, and the more people there were the more rules. In English and in Spanish the notices read, "It is forbidden to walk on the grass." "Dogs must be kept on leash." "No games with balls."

Linda and Sarah turned from one of the subsidiary paths into a main one which was a short cut between the town center and the street that led crookedly toward the docks. And there, immediately in front of her, Linda saw Helen. Helen Shawcross, one of the old school friends who had written and then ceased to do so. As with Mrs. Sarmiento the recognition was instinctive rather than rational. Fifteen years was a long time and Helen had changed quite as much as, even more than Mrs. Sarmiento. But here the change was for the worse. Helen looked thin, harassed, shabby. Imagine Helen Shawcross shabby!

Helen gave no sign of recognition, but that was not surprising. Linda, returning to her native place might expect to meet a familiar face; Helen, if she ever remembered Linda would think of her as far away. So as they drew near, came face to face, Linda stepped in front of Helen and said, "Helen!" Helen took a side step and walked straight on. But their eyes had met; one split-second glance; recognition, fear, warning.

"How very rude!" Sarah exclaimed. Linda put out her hand and took the child's wrist. The path, being a short cut was well used, people going in both directions.

"But she *cut* you," Sarah said, using the

old-fashioned phrase. "Is it someone you used to know?"

"Perhaps not. I could be mistaken. There was some resemblance."

"She looked very poor," said Sarah, who missed little. "And kind of scared."

"Well, if I were mistaken, my stopping dead in front of her like that would be enough to startle her. Let's think about what we'll have for lunch."

"Chicken gumbo and an enormous sundae," Sarah said promptly. She was temporarily diverted but halfway through the meal she said, "Are you worried, Linda?"

"No. What makes you think that?"

"You aren't eating much and you look very serious. Are you brooding about that woman?"

"Why should I? It was my mistake."

"Then why did you nip me?"

"Nip you? I took you by the wrist to pull you out of the way of the people who were just behind her."

Sarah made a curious sound. Accepting? Denying? Dismissing? And proceeded to tackle her sundae. Linda sat and thought about Helen. About the days when to be asked to spend a weekend at Winchester, as the Shawcross plantation was called, had seemed as near to heaven on earth as a child could imagine. The great comfortable house, the happy-go-lucky atmosphere; the dogs, the horses, even the freedom from such small domestic tasks as devolved upon a growing girl in a one-servant doctor's household where her mother answered the door and the telephone, and worked in the little dispensary and very often did first aid as well. It had been impossible to keep a dog there; they had tried twice. In the end both — though of different breeds and temperaments — had turned savage and bitten patients. Linda's father had said, "It is quite hopeless; somebody comes with a boil to be lanced and gets a great lump bitten out of his calf." Linda's mother had said, "I believe people *kick* them. They really have no idea about how to treat animals." They had tried cats; three in rapid succession, a gray, a black, a tortoiseshell. To each in turn Linda had given her heart. Each in turn had vanished, lost, stolen or strayed. She had been about ten when coming into the room she had heard the tag end of a conversation. ". . . into the stew pot, I am convinced," her mother said. "Well, it is understandable; they're all suffering from protein deficiency," her father said with his usual tolerance.

Helen had seemed so enviable. Helen now thin, shabby and frightened. Of what?

"And what shall we do now?" Sarah asked. "Look around the shops?"

"If you like."

The shops, when Linda had been Sarah's age, had been a wonderland, too, on those rare visits. They were still bright and attractive, in a way, but there was a kind of garishness and everything seemed very expensive. The English pound sign had vanished, replaced by the dollar, but whereas the true dollar, American currency, went about three and a half to the pound, the Santa Marian dollar was five and a half; and even when one had done the mental arithmetic, a pair of shoes, worth three pounds and marked twenty dollars seemed costly. Some prices were even more inflated.

*   *   *

"You both look beautiful," Mrs. Gordon said. She was feeling beautiful herself. A visit to the hairdresser always gave her a boost. Mr. Gordon looked at the three female creatures for whom he was responsible and was well satisfied. All happy, all contented, all well looked after; what more could any man ask?

5

"NO, I never went inside it," Linda said, answering Mr. Gordon's question. "The governor held receptions — always a huge one for New Year to which my parents were invited. My father always went so grudgingly, he thought every kind of social activity a waste of time. My mother thought everything was so beautiful. She would tell me about it."

And now, indeed, everything did seem much as it had been described to a wondering child. The vast vaulted hall, the mounting stairs, up and up between the tubs of flowering plants. But now no footmen in quaint, eighteenth-century dress. Soldiers everywhere. Fernandez had come to power through a military coup and this was a military regime. And although by his own wish, Fernandez was referred to as president not general, on this purely civic occasion he was in uniform too, the now familiar khaki and black. Apart from the insignia of rank he was indistinguishable from the others; and except that he had filled out a bit, not much changed from the young soldier who had haunted the kitchen in the old days.

"Mr. and Mrs. Gordon ... Miss Ransom," intoned the officer at the doorway.

"Good-evening. I am happy to see you, Mrs. Gordon.

"Good-evening, Mr. Gordon, I am happy to see you." Polite, mechanical, correct.

To Linda he said, "Miss Ransom. It gives me great pleasure to welcome you back to Santa Maria." And that was a genuine greeting, to which she could only reply with a smile for by that time she had seen and identified the woman by his side.

Yesterday Helen Shawcross, shabby and scared. Today Dolores Heredia y Heredia, gleaming white satin, diamonds. A hand in a white kid elbow-length glove.

The pressure of the crowd behind them moved them on.

Mr. Gordon said, holding his wife by the elbow, "There, now you have done your duty and if there's nowhere to sit we'll stay for ten minutes and no more." There were in fact plenty of places to sit; high-backed couches, covered with crimson velvet, all along one wall.

"Darling, once you sit down at a party you're done for," Mrs. Gordon said; but she allowed herself to be led toward the couches. The "done for" rule might apply to most people, but not to her, George would see to that. At such affairs he always made little safaris, and brought back his trophies, anybody he thought was interesting or amusing. And although he was a thickset man he had a wonderful way of slipping through a crowd. "Let me go ahead," he'd say and, without pushing or treading on toes, he would make a path, which she had only to follow.

Linda was following too, when one of the soldier-waiters stepped in front of her, offering a tray of champagne glasses, the wine gently bubbling. She took one and behind Mrs. Gordon's back the crowd closed in, so that for a moment she stood there as completely isolated as one could only be in a throng composed of people already in groups, or moving steadily towards a given objective. Then Angus Hamilton said, "Hullo, Linda, I've been looking out for you." He was not alone.

Two girls, one short and dark, one tall and fair. "Miss Poppy Sarmiento. Miss Isabel Grant. Miss Linda Ransom." Poppy Sarmineto said, unsmiling, "How do you do." Very correct and formal, not unlike the president. Isabel Grant smiled and said, "Hullo, I've been hoping to meet you somewhere. I'd have rung up but I thought you should have time to settle in before I bothered you. I'm at the hospital."

"I should have said, Dr. Grant," Angus said with an apologetic grin. Poppy Sarmiento, with the making-the-most-of-it gesture of a woman meaning to call attention to herself, fumbled in her sequined bag, produced a cigarette case, also sequined and offered it. "No, of course you don't, Isabel. Linda ? Angus ?"

"Not that make," he said. "Linda, say Thank you nicely and put it back. Have one of these. How anybody can smoke those and remain conscious, beats me."

"It is a question of what one is accustomed to," Poppy said. Taking a light from the lighter which he had taken from his pocket, together with a packet of ordinary English cigarettes, she put her hand around his wrist. Her hands were pretty, plump, the color of milky coffee, every finger ending in a perfect, curved nail, painted the dark red that matched her dress, her lipstick and her name. And her scent, of which Linda had not been conscious until the cigarette was burning — heavy and sweet. Poppy! Opium, or some derivative of it?

Poppy with an adept movement, rearranged the foursome, so that she and Angus made one pair, the other two girls another. Isabel Grant said, "You won't remember me, of course; I'm years older and was sent to school in the States. But I had the most sincere admiration for your father — in fact it is because of him that I am a doctor, now. My father was ill for so many years — multiple sclerosis — and your father was kinder than God. You see we were so poor. If we'd had to pay fees and charges for medicine I should have had no education at all." She spoke with sincerity and frankness. She was not pretty, her face was too long, her forehead too high, but her eyes were beautiful, especially now, alight with enthusiasm.

"It is very pleasant to hear one's father spoken of in that way. And to know that he is not forgotten."

"I was absolutely disgusted by the decision not to name the hospital after him," Isabel said, quite another emotion brightening her eyes. "It was all part of . . . Well, never mind. However, the moment I heard that you were back I tackled the management committee and you are to be invited to make an official tour of the place and to be lunched, as the Americans say, by the minister of health."

"What did I ever do to deserve such an ordeal?" Linda asked, only half joking.

"It will at least serve to remind people of the name, and of what they owe. Such things have been too readily forgotten."

"And what is the latest news of the Demon Child," Angus asked, addressing Linda over Poppy's shoulder. "Is she going to gatecrash again tonight?"

"I think transport would present a problem," Linda said.

He told the story of the purser's party.

"And you have to look after this spoiled brat?" Poppy asked with a look that held insolence as well as feigned pity. How times had changed! For just as Helen had seemed enviable to Linda, so Linda had appeared enviable to Poppy.

"Good-evening again," said a low vibrant voice, addressing them as a group. Everybody said, "Good-evening, madam." The president's wife was performing the second round of her duty — a personal word with as many people as possible. Gracious, without smiling; except for the dark eyes and the cloud of black hair, a figure that might have been fashioned out of snow and ice and animated by some hidden mechanism, Dolores hoped that Angus was enjoying the laboratory facilities, was glad that Dr. Grant had managed to give herself a free evening, congratulated Miss Sarmiento on her latest promotion and then turned to Linda and with a movement much like Poppy's earlier on, separated her from the group. She said, "I hope it has been a happy homecoming, Miss Ransom . . ." and then, lips scarcely moving, "Follow me out, unostentatiously." She passed on.

"I must just see if Mrs. Gordon . . ." Linda said.

The Spanish governors had been content with the vast vaulted hall and a few ground floor rooms opening off it; the French governors had been responsible for the building up and the building out, and the English governors had had the sense to leave well enough alone. In this great room five French windows stood open to a terrace overlooking the garden. Dolores went out through the one at the extreme left and Linda, wondering if she looked as furtive as she felt, counted ten and then followed. The terrace was lighted, but dimly, and after the blaze of the chandeliers, it seemed dark. Dolores had chosen the left-hand window, so it was reasonable to think that she had gone that way. She was waiting by another French window at the extreme end of the terrace. "Come in," she said. She closed the window behind her and drew the heavy white and gold curtains. "Nobody will disturb us here. I am allowed twenty minutes. Do sit down." She lowered herself, rather carefully on to a white and gold daybed and lay flat. "I have a disability," she said. "I cannot stand for much more than an hour at a time. Well, Linda? You are surprised? Shocked?"

"Surprised — yes, I had no idea. Shocked — should I be?"

Yet shock was the correct word. Dolores Heredia y Heredia, the daughter of the proudest family of Santa Maria married to Jose Fernandez.

Nobody at the convent had envied Dolores, brought to school each morning, collected each afternoon in a carriage, in which rode a stern-faced old woman, her duenna. She had been betrothed, at the age of ten, to a remote cousin whom she had never seen, and probably would not see until he arrived from Cuba for the wedding. The Geredia family had survived, under the French, under the English, by making outward adjustments, bowing to every wind of change, but by preserving, intact and immutable, the whole mystique of traditional family life — a powerful network. Spaniards and Frenchmen, Frenchmen and Englishmen might shed their ordinary common blood in order to gain a bit of territory, but always, somewhere, on another level there was a beautiful woman or a clever man ready to put in the necessary word that would gain the necessary immunity until things settled down again.

"It was not a thing I could write about," Dolores said. "There are various forms of death. I died one of them when Fernandez made his coup. And you have no right to judge me. You were playing *hockey* in a place called Felixstowe. And although what got into the papers made it sound spontaneous, unanimous, a peaceful take-over, it was far from that. Even the army was not solidly behind Fernandez. We had four days of civil war about which nothing was ever heard. The English did not wish to hear. Santa Maria was independent and must settle things in her own way." Abruptly Dolores sat up, reached for a gold box, offered Linda a cigarette, took one herself, flicked a gold lighter. She smoked in an agitated way. "The winning side, Linda, does not in these civilized days, take open vengeance. My brother had fought — on the losing side; he was wounded, and detained. You can imagine how and in what circumstances. It was a life for a life, Linda. Fernandez had seen me somewhere — in church I can only suppose — and taken a fancy. And he needed a wife who could handle affairs like this," she jerked her head in the direction of the noise, just audible. "I will be fair. No pressure was put upon me by the family. I made my choice, but it was a hard bargain. And it did no good. Felipez *was* released, he *had* the best medical attention. He lived six months. The day he died my father shot himself. That is the kind of thing that does not get into the papers."

"I am most terribly sorry, Dolores."

"You must not pity me, Linda. I am relatively well off. Hundreds suffered more and are still suffering. You remember Helen Shawcross?"

"I do indeed. I was about to ask. I think I saw her yesterday."

"Both her brothers were killed in the streets — on the losing side. Winchester was taken by the government, all very correct, compulsory purchase. An agricultural institute *was* needed. There was pretence at valuation — half a dollar an acre or some such nonsense. Enough, anyway for Helen and her mother to come into Port Philip and start a small private hotel. But, and here is the point, Linda," Dolores stubbed out her half-smoked cigarette, lighted another, "once you're on the wrong side you're on the wrong side. Old Mrs. Shawcross had kept photographs, you know the style, "This is the house I used to live in," "This is the horse my husband bred that won the Kentucky Derby." That kind of nonsense. The tourists lapped it up, of course. Always this harking back by those who have little to hark back to. Romantic . . . Anyway," she glanced at her diamond-encrusted watch, "word got about. Subversive. A man from the ministry of health went along and said the drains were a danger to health and closed the place down. The last I heard of Helen she was working in a cafe near the docks." That fitted. Helen was hurrying through the public gardens toward Rope Walk.

"And you could do nothing?" Linda asked.

"No. For one thing the situation is not so static as it may seem to you, just arrived. Pro-Fernandez, anti-Fernandez. Not physically; *mentally*. And for another thing, people like Helen — and there are a lot of them — would like nothing better than a chance to spit in my face. To them I am the renegade of renegades. The traitor. Can you see now why I did not write to you, playing hockey in a place called Felixstowe. And to make matters worse — I have no wish to insult you, Linda, but times have changed so much. . . . Did you ever sleep with a man?"

"No." And no virtue in that; it had been a matter of never the time and the place and the loved one altogether. "I have wanted to."

"It has an effect," Dolores said, looking at her watch again. "I hated him. My very blood revolted. Submitting to the enemy . . . But he was kind. Gentle. He wears a public face . . . and most of what has been done has been done under that public face, confident, arrogant. But there is another side to him; the little boy, not lost, little boy dressed up, pushed on to the stage, playing the part he wished for but was not fully prepared for. . . . I have a certain fondness. Not love . . . But there again I was better off than many; it is doubtful if I should have loved Ferdinand, to whom I was betrothed. It was easier for me than for a young woman not reared to expect an arranged marriage, because I already knew . . ." For a moment her look softened. Then she stubbed out that cigarette and again looked at her watch. She said, as though contradicting some statement. "Fernandez is honest, but he cannot rule alone and all members of the government are not . . . Now I must return to my post. I shall see you from time to time, Linda, on official occasions. It would be unwise of me to appear to cherish any link with the past."

She got up and studied herself in the full-length looking glass, smoothed her satin skirt, touched her hair, reassuming her official look. "I shall go that way," she said, nodding toward an inner door. "You go by the terrace." She put her hand on Linda's arm. "Seeing you, being able to speak from the heart for once, has done me a great deal of good. One word of warning, Linda. Don't join *anything*, however harmless it may appear. Not even a musical society!"

The conversation had left Linda with a curious feeling, as though her skin did not quite fit. Too many things had been left unsaid; too much of what had been said was not cheerful hearing. As she stepped out of the window of Dolores' bedroom she was a little disconcerted to see a man's figure, halfway between that window and one by which she had left the ball room. Watching? Ridiculous! Yet Dolores had been deliberately secretive and somehow the whole trend of her talk . . . It was only her imagination that made her think that the man might be spying, but it was a fancy strong enough to make her wonder whether to turn and reenter the bedroom and return to the party that way, or whether she could slip past him, unobserved. She went forward.

"I was waiting for you," Angus said. "I saw you vanish and when you didn't come back I thought maybe you were escaping from Poppy. And then you weren't here. So I waited. Look . . ." He had brought out two glasses of champagne and set them on the top of the stone balustrade. He did not ask where she had been.

From the garden below the fragrance of night-scented flowers came up; beyond the garden the lights of the town shone. Windows in no pattern, street lamps defining the streets, straight, crooked, and far away the semicircular curve of the bay. Helen in a dockside cafe! Alan and Roger Shawcross both dead. Brooding did no good.

"I like Isabel Grant," she said, seizing on the first thing that came into her mind. "How did you meet her?"

"Not in the happiest of circumstances . . ." He seemed to be brooding too. "Place called Winchester."

"The agricultural college?"

"So called. Well, it is, in part. There are some students, and some animals — that's why I went there. But really it's . . . Oh never mind. Let's talk about something else."

"You tell me what's on your mind. It's therapeutic. I met a woman, quite recently who talked to me in the most *un*cheerful way, but she said she felt better for it."

"What was her *un*cheerful theme?"

"Marital problems, largely. Come on, Angus, you tell me. Did you find some animals all skin and bone?" She knew that he had a very soft, almost a neurotically soft, spot for animals and she knew the typical Spanish-West Indian attitude toward them.

"God no! I could have done something about that; vested with government authority. Even my boss wouldn't have argued. . . . No, the animals were in good shape. It was the people . . ."

"The students?"

"God no!" he said again. "They're fine, having the time of their lives. Linda . . . Winchester is a sort of labor camp.

They don't *call* it that. They say 'corrective', but its the same thing. Anybody puts a foot wrong, says an unwelcome word, six months at Winchester will correct him or her. Death the cure for all ills, even political. They do all the work, they're practically starved. They've got every deficiency disease known; and the absolutely bloody thing is the humbug! Dr. Grant from the fine new hospital, monthly inspection. All fine and dandy. Poor old girl, I came across her crying her eyes out, leaning against her car. I was bloody near crying myself. But what can you do?"

She had heard that question often enough. "What can you do?" her father had asked, coming in from a breach delivery of some prostitute's eleventh child, a decent working man's fourteenth, or from some old man or woman, pellagra. *What can you do?*"

She said, "Nothing. Except, as somebody said, tend your garden. On the whole, I think, I hope, that things are better. There is a kind of overall balance. There were some very bad things in the old days. The beggars have gone now, and the brothels and the men running down to the docks, undercutting each other by two-pence a day. And there is this to remember, Angus . . . there is a kind of *choice* now. I mean, in the old days, deprivation was forced on people. If, as you say, those now in the corrective camp put a foot wrong, or said something . . . they did *choose* to do so. They *knew* what they were about and what was likely to happen. Can you see the difference?"

"You're dead right," he said after thinking this over. "And right about talking things over. A different slant. I do feel better."

"I'm glad." But she was aware that she had been indulging in sophistry — up to a point. What choice had Helen had? Or Dolores? "By the way," she said, "have you been asked to join things?"

"Dozens. There's a kind of rotary, a kind of freemasonry, a musical, a literary, an amateur dramatic society and several crank things, several clubs."

"Did you?"

"Did I what?"

"Join any?"

"No. To tell you the truth I'm a natural loner, a born nonjoiner. . . ."

"Oh, *there* you are," Mr. Gordon said. "I've been keeping an eye . . . She's bearing up marvelously but enough is enough and I think she's had it. See you on Thursday, Hamilton. Until then . . ."

* * *

"It was a delightful party," Mrs. Gordon said, sinking into her seat and suffering a kind of collapse, not a deflated balloon for she had not been inflated, more as though she had been filleted.

"You talked too much," her husband said, bearing down on the accelerator. In fact he was proud of her; she might be restricted to one glass of champagne, and unable to stand up for long at a stretch, but she was always animated and seemed to know just what to say to everyone. "And how did you get on, Linda? Sorry I had to interrupt your balcony scene."

"I made a discovery. The president's wife is a girl I was with at school. I'd imagined her married and living in Cuba." She told them a little about the Heredia y Heredia family.

"Rich?" Mr. Gordon asked.

"We always thought so."

"That'd explain the diamonds, then," he said, rather as if the jewels had mystified him. "Fernandez struck me as having his head screwed on the right way and I must say the diamonds struck me as being a bit much, with so much poverty still about."

"Darling, you were simply jealous. Just because I wasn't glittering like a Christmas tree," Mrs. Gordon said, teasingly, lovingly.

"You looked every bit as well as she did," he said with that note of aggression in his voice. "And a damned sight more lively! I only mentioned the diamonds because . . . well, Fernandez is supposed to be a man of the people and he seems to be an unassuming sort of chap . . . And there must have been about seven hundred and fifty people there. Champagne flowing. I can see that it doesn't quite button up in some people's eyes. Down at the factory" — he never could accustom himself to the word mill — "the average wage is around six dollars. Not much over a pound. Average, that is, some get less." He had a mild obsession with money, enjoyed speculating about other people's incomes and doing sums in his head.

"It's a kind of hangover," Linda said, "from the great days of Empire. Governors had splendid parties, therefore the president must. Prestige. If he'd clamped down and served cheap, native stuff, rum and lime, a lot of people, people who'd supported him, would feel, well, disappointed. Not on the gravy train after all."

"Yes," Mr. Gordon said, dragging the word out meditatively, "I can see that."

They were home.

Whoever had planned the Executives' Paradise had borne in mind that when it rained in Santa Maria, it rained. The garage had a door to the kitchen. They went in quietly in order not to wake Theresa who occupied what was almost a self-contained flat, a bedroom and bathroom opening out of the kitchen by another door.

"Linda'll bring your milk," Mr. Gordon said in a whisper that sounded like a stage aside. "Come on, into bed with you." Linda took the milk from the refrigerator, poured a glass and put out lights.

On the landing, Mr. Gordon, wearing his worried look, stood outside Sarah's door. He said, conspiratorily, "Locked!

She's never before . . . Thank you, Linda."
He said the last words in an ordinary voice,
took the milk and went into their bedroom.
"Here you are, my dear, I'm not quite sure
if I put off the light in the garage, I'll just
slip down . . ." He came out on to the landing, closing the door behind him. "I just
thought I'd peep in," he said, "and the door
was locked. Why would she do that?"

"I don't know," Linda said. "But what
I do know . . ." She reached past him, took
the key from her own bedroom door,
pushed it in, turned it very gently, heard
the key on the inside fall; turned it more
purposefully and opened the door. Enough
light came from the landing to show Sarah,
sound asleep, looking like a crop-headed
angel.

"Well, that's all right then," Mr. Gordon
said. "Thank you. Thank you, Linda. I
thought . . . but never mind . . . Good-night,
my dear. Sleep well."

                    *   *   *

"I didn't mean anybody to know," Sarah
said. "I'd set my alarm, in case I went to
sleep, though I didn't think I should. I
meant to open the door before you were

back. I know that Daddy likes to look in. But you were a bit early, weren't you?"

"Just a bit. But what made you lock the door?"

"Well, I know it sounds silly. Theresa frightened me. And I know that it was silly to lock the door. No guard, really, but it made me feel safer."

"Against what?" The thing which sometimes looked, mischievously or defiantly, from Sarah's eyes looked now, but secretively.

"I am ashamed of myself for letting her scare me. Especially now. By night — and alone in the house with her — it seemed different. And if you ever all go out again I *shall* go to Ian's. Shall we get on, now?"

"Was it anything she *said*?" Linda persisted. "Remember, Sarah, I grew up here. We had a cook who used to tell me tales that made my hair stand on end."

"Then you know," Sarah said, with an air of finality.

"I wonder if the tales are the same," Linda said cunningly. "The one I minded most was about a zombie."

"The Walking Dead!" Sarah said, falling into the trap. "I didn't mind that; it isn't so different from Lazarus. Theresa knows worse ones."

*   *   *

"I din mean no harm," Theresa said. "I set Little Miss's supper in the dining room, but that don't suit. She brung it to the kitchen and there she set. I tell her, 'Time for bed,' I tell her, but she don't pay me no mind. So she set and maybe I did tell her a tale or two. I don't know no pretty tales. Only know tales my mammy tell me, her mammy tell her. I din mean no harm."

The main omission from this account was Theresa's reason for wanting Sarah out of the way.

"Oh no, I don't for a moment suppose you did, Theresa," Linda said. "But you see, tales that you and I grew up with and that did us no harm," tact must be my middle name! "could frighten a little girl straight out from England."

"Little girl from England," Theresa said darkly, "should go to bed. Nine o'clock, like her mammy say. Like her teacher say." That was a sly dig!

"Well, I don't suppose it will happen that we shall all be out together again. But

86

if we should, please remember, Theresa, no more tales."

Mr. Gordon, she knew would have carried more weight, spoken with greater authority, but he had enough to worry him.

6

"YOU'RE none of you old enough to see things in proper prospective." Mr. Lopez said, looking at Linda, Isabel and Angus. "I am. And when you think of the progress, the innovations of the last half century, you see the impossibility of taking the leap in a few years. And the craziest, the most blatantly self-hampering act ever passed was the one about Spanish in schools. You take a country," he said, gesticulating with his coffee spoon, "with a very low level of education — less than one percent ever had more than primary education; you build fine new schools, say secondary education for all and university for those fit for it. And then you say teachers must be bilingual. Suicide."

"I once knew a women," Linda said, "who was at school in Kilkenny when the Irish came into their own. From one day to another all teaching had to be done in Erse. Her first lesson that day was algebra. Imagine!"

"But, at least," Mr. Lopez said, contentiously, "Erse was alive, still spoken in some homes — otherwise such a change would not have been feasible. In Santa Maria only about three percent of the population had any Spanish at all. I was born here, I bear a Spanish name. I didn't know a word of the language until I went to spend a long holiday with some relatives in Madrid. I was fourteen — old enough to take interest in pretty girls. I learned at a phenomenal rate. Little, little dreaming of what use it would be to me half a century later."

"That act," Isabel said, "was designed to make the teaching profession a closed shop."

"Precisely. But a closed shop keeps people out and in this case the people excluded were the very ones we wanted. I am not to blame for the lack of promising pupils on the science side." That was the kick-off point of this conversation. "There are so few teachers; science and the gift of tongues seldom go together, and boys — girls, too," he said, out of courtesy to Dr. Grant, "who should be in the laboratories, spend two hours a day learning Spanish grammar and studying Cervantes in the original." He waved his spoon so violently that it flew through the air and landed in Linda's lap. "The president himself speaks Spanish about as well as I speak Latin — which is not well! Indeed, it is said that his purpose in marrying Madame was to improve his vocabulary. And this stupid, outdated nationalism has done more than cripple education. It has ensured that all the real power is concentrated in the hands of one small group, all of the same origin. Men who were attached to, often in a very menial capacity, those estates where Spanish was still spoken. I talk too much," he said, accepting back his spoon, "but this I must say. They, being the most downtrodden, were naturally the strongest supporters of the revolution. They may have earned their present prominence, but I for one do not exactly relish serving under a minister of education who was bookkeeper on the Heredia y Heredia estate."

"You," Isabel Grant said, "should be a little careful about statements like that, Mr. Lopez."

"I know. I know. As a rule I am careful; but here, amongst friends — at least I hope, friends. And with wine in me. And there is one comfort. They have not yet bugged private apartments. I suspect that is because there is an insufficient number of engineers with the necessary skill."

It had started off as an ordinary dinner party. "I never had a housewarming," Angus said, "and my old Maria is always complaining that I don't entertain. She thinks that a reflection on her cooking. I'll ask Isabel — you liked one another, didn't you? And the head of the high school. We made contact over a boy who does most earnestly want to be a veterinary but can hardly spell cat. But I liked the old boy, he isn't smeared with the all's-right-in-Santa Maria treacle."

Unmarried men, under contract, were allocated flats in a tall concrete-and-glass tower not far from the hospital; they were also allotted one serving woman, old, or old-looking. Linda had been once in Angus' flat before and thought it a cheerless apartment, not particularly well kept, no flowers, none of those little personal touches which say home. Tonight it was much improved; evidently the prospect of company had inspired Maria. Every surface that could be polished shone, the dining table was covered with a lacy cloth and had flowers on it; there were more flowers on the coffee table. And the meal had been delicious; pumpkin soup, fried conch, and bananas baked with rum and grated coconut. Now they were drinking strong, black coffee and a sweet liqueur with a rum base and a pineapple flavor.

Until one ill-judged remark had started Mr. Lopez on his policitical harangue it had been such a good party that Angus had been encouraged to plan another, asking Mr. and Mrs. Gordon who had twice entertained him, and were as kind and pleasant as possible. But there was something — not the age gap — Mr. Lopez was far older than either of them. It was their relationship to Linda, almost parental, so that in their presence he felt as though they were sizing him up. There was also their tacit assumption that the relationship between him and Linda was considerably more advanced than it actually was. He liked her very much, he'd liked her the first moment he'd seen her and nothing had happened to diminish that liking. But he had his own views; he did not intend to get married before he was thirty and he did not intend to mess about with a nice girl like Linda. Nature had kindly provided plenty of the other kind. . .

"I don't want to break up this delicious party, Angus," Isabel said, "but duty calls."

"I will walk across with you," Mr. Lopez said. "It was indeed a delightful dinner and the time has flown. I had no idea that it . . ."

The telephone made its particularly raucous, West Indian noise. Angus answered it, sounding for a moment exactly like Mr. Gordon. Snappy. "Yes . . . Yes . . . No . . . No . . . What?" Then he said, "All right." Turning back to his guests but dropping his role of host, he said, "Typical. They choose to ring up at eleven o'clock at night to tell me they've found the parcel I've been badgering them about for a week. And I can have it if I go down and identify it and write my name twenty times. Sorry, but it's stuff I want. Stuff I've been waiting for."

Isabel said, "We were on our way. . . ."

Linda said, "Customs office? I'll run you down. It would save time."

"Yes, it would. Thanks!"

Mr. Gordon had adhered to his intention to buy another car, and it had arrived, bright, and shining. A Seagull, not a large car but luxurious, a car in which Linda could drive Juliet to wherever she needed to go. And Mr. Parker's warning about import duty had been unjustified; so had his warning about damage. The Seagull had slipped into Santa Maria like a seagull. The bit about spare parts had been nonsense, too. Mr. Gordon had checked before placing his order. Anything that a defective Seagull needed could be supplied within twenty-four hours from St. Agnes, just across the water.

The Seagull stood in that part of the enclosure before the flats, labeled, in the prevalent English, the useless Spanish, "Visitors Only". The cars of the flat residents had less room, pressed together between the stilts on which the block was reared. That was why Linda had said that it would save time to use it, rather than Angus' own car.

"You drive this?" Isabel asked.

"Yes. It was very fortunate. . . . I actually learned to drive on a Seagull." Long ago and far away, in a distant summer, a summer full of excitement and promise, but shriveling as it bloomed. Charles saying, "Darling!" Put it away, all over and done with, best forgotten.

"Yes. Mr. Gordon bought it for his wife, a birthday present. But she does not drive and I do. And I am allowed to use it . . . like tonight."

"It's pretty conspicuous," Isabel said, rather critically. It was designed to be conspicuous. The shining silver gull poised on the bonnet, beak cleaving the air, wings streamlined by the wind, was alone sufficient to mark it out. In addition Mr. Gordon had chosen white, with blue upholstery.

Isabel's remark puzzled Linda; it smacked of envy, alien, she would have thought, to the other girl's nature.

"It's pretty, period," she said, lightly.

With renewed thanks and more good-nights Isabel and Mr. Lopez walked away and Linda drove down to the quayside.

"I'll wait for you," she said.

"I'd sooner you didn't. I may well be half an hour, you know how they keep you hanging about. It won't be a heavy parcel and the walk back will do me good."

"Well, if I'm here when you come out . . ." she said, thinking that she might be. "If not, good-night and thanks for a lovely dinner."

"You get along," he said. "This isn't a particularly salubrious area, and as Isabel said, this is a pretty conspicuous vehicle."

To humor him she set the car in motion, then as he vanished into the complex of buildings on the seaward side of the wide esplanade, she drove more and more slowly and finally halted again. "A cafe near the docks," Dolores had said. There were a great many, ranging from the supremely elegant Cafe Continentale which was part of the big hotel, built for tourists and V.I.P.s, which stood on high ground at the north side of the bay, to dirty little dives frequented by dockers and the more poorly paid members of freighter crews. And dock might mean anything within two or three blocks inland. The hope of finding Helen seemed remote and frail. She had made one attempt, a hasty reconnaissance on the day when, driving the Seagull for the first time, she had brought Mrs. Gordon and Sarah on a shopping expedition. It had been hasty because Mr. Gordon had said, "An hour is the most she can stand. She fell down in a dead faint in Harrod's. So I trust you to keep an eye . . ."

That one hour had been, by the process of elimination, helpful. Most of the cafes were strictly family affairs — man and wife, mother and daughter. By the time she had realised that there were only about five places large enough to employ hired help it was time to go back and collect her passengers.

Of the five the Velasquez was the largest, and one which remained open all night. It was also the one which had made some endeavour to conceal a fundamental sleaziness; it had been recently painted — pale mauve and an orangy red, a combination curiously popular with a certain section of Santa Marians. Bad paint, powdery. And though outside the door there were tubs — striped mauve and orangy red — planted with flowering shrubs, salmon pink oleanders, they had a neglected air. The name across the front and the entrance itself was lit by tiny electric light bulbs, similar to those used to illuminate Christmas trees. A third of them were out of action.

Linda ran the car past the entrance, into the shadow and stopped. And sat.

Mustering courage?

For what?

There is no law, so far as I know, against going into a public place. Anywhere where Helen can *work* surely I can enter as a customer. Surely.

But in fact she was not so sure. You grew up, beginning in a colony, proceeding to England . . . where the Union Jack flew all men were equal and free despite the economic differences. A false assurance, its fallacy shown once old Granny Britannia had handed over her authority.

The door under the incomplete arch of lights opened; two men came out and walked away.

Why do I hesitate? Because I am a coward and my nerve has been broken — that man flinging beer in Angus' face; Helen's scared look, everything Dolores said, little by little adding up to make me afraid to walk into this not entirely disreputable-looking place and asking, "Does Miss Shawcross work here?" She had made up her mind to do it, had her hand on the handle of the car door when, just across the path, a door in the dark building opened, an oblong of light out of which a woman walked, was plainly visible for two seconds and then invisible as the door closed.

Linda said, "Helen!" into the gloom. "It's Linda."

The car door was snatched open from outside and Helen shot into the vacant seat, bringing with her a strong smell of hot oil and garlic and spice.

"Drive away," she said. "Drive away, anywhere."

The Seagull started at a touch. Linda felt Helen lift the pretty gauzy scarf — all one needed in the way of a wrap in this warm climate — from her shoulders and drape it over her own head.

"You always were a bf," Helen said, in the language of their past. "Coming to meet me in this thing! Why not a fire engine? Go left here, and left again." It seemed to be some kind of siding, unlighted and completely deserted.

"I so wanted to see you, Helen. Didn't you want to see me?"

"If you'd got any sense you'd have known by the way I walked past you that

99

day. How did you know where I worked, anyway?"

"I didn't. It was the purest chance, though I was just making up my mind to come in and ask. . . . Somebody said you worked at a cafe not far from the docks and I thought the Velasquez looked possible."

"My God! What an escape!"

"But why, Helen? What is it all about?"

"I'm in trouble enough, without consorting with a friend from the past — straight out from England. Relict of better days. Backward looking. Subversive! And it wouldn't do you any good either. Mark that! Look, you got a cigarette on you? Good. Let's descend from this shining chariot and find somewhere to sit, and I will tell you all."

She drew on her cigarette in a famished way, and grew calmer. "Did your informant give you a full case history?"

"No details. Just that you'd been cheated out of Winchester and then cheated out of your hotel."

"You remember Ma?"

"Of course I do. She used to be so kind to me."

"Losing Alan and Roger — and Winchester — turned her senile, Linda. She wasn't dotty, she knew what had happened, but she just would not be careful. We had a pretty good type of guest — considering the size of our place — and of course they lapped up her talk. Ye goode olde days and would you like to see some photographs? It did no harm and they liked it — Americans, I mean; it gave them something to talk about. Then some blithering idiot thought she'd be a crusader. She went home and wrote letters to papers — An Island Eden with a Serpent as President. You know the form. It was sensational. She'd pinched one of Ma's photographs and taken some of her own. Ma taking the prize at some dressage event, Ma coming home from market laden like a pack donkey. It never fails, from rags to riches in one generation is a tale, from riches to rags in a couple of years is a supertale. Linda, Ma and I bloody nearly went back to Winchester in a way Mrs. Crusader didn't visualize! If I hadn't been damned smart . . . Anyway, our drains went wrong and we were out of business and we have been under suspicion ever since. That finished Ma, she is now dotty as a coot, can't tell

Monday from Tuesday. . . . But that's enough about me. Let's talk about you. What the hell brought you back here? Couldn't you read between the lines and know when you were well off. Never mind; don't bother to answer. Just listen to me. Because I *know*. You get going while the going's good. You have a passport?"

"Yes, but . . ."

"But me no buts, as somebody said. Where I work I hear things. Something is boiling up, Linda. And what the end may be, nobody knows. The truth is Fernandez set himself to walk in the middle of the road, and anybody in the middle of the road is vulnerable from *both* sides. Maybe it wasn't accident that I came out of that door when I did. . . . I was always fond of you, Linda. I admit just now I was furious with you for being so bloody stupid . . . but I don't think anybody saw and it may have been meant. You scarper off, Lindy-loo." The old pet name.

"But I engaged myself for a year."

"Forget about it. Go sick. Have a nervous breakdown. Anything. Just get away while your passport holds. Lindy-loo, I do mean that, seriously. Fernandez clapped down on passports and whoever wins, left or right, will copy his methods. God!" Helen said violently, "I thought I didn't care what happened to anybody except me and Ma and I thought I had that organized. Now there's you! And you think I'm dotty, too. I'm not, you know. What with one thing and another I'm about as well informed . . . but nobody can tell how the cat will jump. Do please listen to me. Make some excuse . . ." She bit her thumb, an old habit. "I know a man in Cables; if I ask him he'll send you a cable from any place you like to name — 'Come at once Aunt Edna dying and asking for you.' Fool anybody! Linda, if I do that, will you go? Get on any old tub, banana boat, anything and make for Belle Isle. They have an airport, so that would look natural. . . ." She put her hand on Linda's; it was a hand that had only just finished washing dishes — wrinkled and damp as a washerwoman's.

"I should have to think about it, Helen. The Gordons have been so extremely kind to me. . . ."

"Oh, don't talk like a bloody fool," Helen snatched her hand away. Then in a different voice she said, "Well, I have warned you. And I'll get the cable to you — it may take a week. You've had your chance, if you don't take it it's your own affair. Only don't come near me. Don't write to me or anything. We'll probably meet at Winchester — one way or another. Good-bye." She jumped up and seemed to vanish into the darkness.

7

CONTRARY to all custom, Mr. Gordon had brought what Sarah called his homework out of the study into the sitting room. He looked up as Linda entered, removed his glasses and rubbed his eyes.

"You'd better ring up your beau," he said. "He rang up half an hour ago and seemed a bit upset to hear that you weren't home. Put him out of his misery." He began to gather his papers together, preparatory to leaving her with the telephone.

"Don't go," she said. "There's nothing private about this. And I would like to speak to you for a minute."

She made the call and Angus sounded relieved and a little curious as to why she should have been late. "I thought perhaps, new car, teething troubles, and a lonely road. To tell you the truth I was just about to mount a search party."

"New cars have to run in. Anyhow, I'm

home and dry. But thanks for the kind thought. Good-night, Angus."

"I'm going to give myself a reward for overtime," Mr. Gordon said, making for the table where the drinks stood. "How about joining me? You looked a bit tired."

That was one of the nice things about the Gordons; they respected one's privacy. Most people would have shown some curiosity about that lost half hour, if only by remarking that she *was* late.

"Thank you," she said and accepted what Mr. Gordon called a lady's measure of whisky, weaker than his own.

"Now," he said, "what is it, my dear? Sarah?"

"No. I'm late because . . ."

"Now, now," he said, "no need for that! You don't have to report." All the same, the Seagull had needed the minimum of running in and had ticked up that specified mileage.

"I met, quite by chance, an old friend, a girl I was at school with. And we had a talk."

"Any why not?"

"She said some rather strange things, Mr. Gordon. I've been thinking all the way home. She spoke as though I had been a fool to come back here and she urged me to leave before trouble broke out. Have you ever heard . . . Do you think there's anything in it ?"

"Do you *seriously* think," he asked, "that I should be sitting here, drinking whisky, with my wife and child asleep upstairs if I thought there was the remotest possibility . . . ?"

"No, of course not. But you might not *know*. . . . That is why I thought I would just mention it, Mr. Gordon. H . . . — my friend is a level-headed kind of girl and she's lived here all her life. She did sound extremely earnest."

"I'd make a guess," he said, "that she's one of those who lost out when Fernandez took over."

"That is quite true."

"Well, she's not the only one. There are quite a number and I have heard all about them. They get together, musical societies, reading circles, sewing bees for all I know, and talk over their grievances and *plot*. It's a futile pastime, but harmless and it keeps them cheerful."

"That's curious," Linda said. "Another

girl I was at school with warned me not to *join* anything, not even a musical society."

"She had good sense. I'd have told you the same if you'd ever shown any inclination. And since we're on the subject, there's another side to it, too. Fernandez went a good deal too far for some people and not nearly far enough for others. *They* have little undercover meetings, too. And *they* plot. It's a pretty usual pattern. Those who lost a sizable cake dream of the days when they'll get it back; those who got a bit of the cake, but less than they'd counted on, dream of the days when they'll have a whole cake. They all get drunk on talk — talk like that can be intoxicating, you know — and they overlook one salient fact; the army is one hundred percent behind Fernandez. And he was shrewd enough to make army and police one and indivisible. I admit the economy is a bit creaky, but it's getting better every day. I don't like to work under our friend Parker. . . . But there again, I see the point. In every key job, the tried, old, faithful friend. These minority groups haven't a hope in hell. No arms for one thing. Don't misunderstand me, I hold no brief for dictatorship, there are some things I am bound to disapprove of; but if you can't have a democracy with three hundred years of experience behind it, the next best thing is a strong dictator with army discipline behind him. Every political experiment needs some discipline — that is why so many of them go wrong."

*   *   *

Isabel Grant's letter was a surprise, coming a week after Angus' party, where they had been on Christian name terms.

Dear Miss Ransom,
I have been obliged to cancel the little drinks party to which I invited you. My training college, on Belle Isle, has arranged a conference for the Easter vacation on the subject Child Health in Relationship to Child Education. Mr. Lopez and I propose to attend and it occurred to me that, since although you work in a private capacity at the moment, having attended such a conference might be of help to you in the future if you ever sought a post in a state school. If you would like to come with us it could easily be arranged. Such conferences are very informal and Belle Isle, being flat,

is warmer than Santa Maria. You would need the minimum of luggage. I know that this is very short notice. Mr. Lopez and I leave on Thursday. But if you will telephone me, at the hospital until eight o'clock, and after that at my home, I will see to everything. I do hope you will be able to get away. Yours sincerely,

Isabel Grant

"Well, of course, if you want to go," Mr. Gordon said. "I suppose that with one thing and another you deserve a bit of a holiday. There's Sarah, of course, but between us we can manage, I suppose. . . ."

"It doesn't strike you as rather a curious letter, Mr. Gordon?"

"No. Should it?" He glanced at it again. "Well, curious in the assumption that having done with us you'd need a job. I'd somehow got the impression that young Hamilton . . . Nothing to do with me," he added hastily. "It's your own life. But what's curious about this invitation?"

"The tone. We met at the president's party; on Christian names from the start, and we have been ever since. Now suddenly so very formal. Oh, I know you think I'm overimaginative. . . . But honestly, Mr. Gordon, this does sound to me like a letter written to be read by somebody else but me. So extremely formal . . . and correct."

"And what's wrong with that? Of course it was meant for other eyes. Mine. I'm looking at it now. If she'd written 'Dear Linda, my boyfriend and I are off on a jaunt. Join us,' it wouldn't have read so well. A lot of young women, closing in for the kill, like to have a girl friend around. Looks better."

"Mr. Lopez is well over sixty, Mr. Gordon."

"Well . . . I can think of another explanation. It was a dictated letter. They always tend to turn out a bit stiff-sounding. I can remember once — Persia I think — I got stung on the hand by a damned great thing like a hornet and had to dictate letters to my wife. You've no idea how tongue-tied I sounded or how stilted they turned out to be. We seem to have wandered from the point. You want Easter off. You take it, you're only young once."

"I haven't the slightest wish to go to some stodgy old conference," Linda said. "I only showed you the letter because . . .

Mr. Gordon, I know you'll think I've got a bee in my bonnet, but when I read this I couldn't help thinking that perhaps yet *another* friend of my friends was offering me an escape route."

"It isn't one bee, dear girl. It's a whole hive. I told you the other night what I feel and what I know about the situation. And even if both your friends are right and there's a bit of rioting over the holiday, it wouldn't touch *us*. We're British subjects, here on contract. I know that doesn't mean what it once did, with a war breaking out over Jenkin's ear or Nobb's nose or some such. But I am convinced that if the extreme left and the extreme right come to blows in the streets of Port Philip, nobody would touch us. For one thing we're too damned indispensable."

"You don't think that it would be nice for us *all* to go Belle Isle for Easter?"

"No. I do not." He held up three of his sensitive, fidgety fingers. "First, because I can't spare the time. Second, there isn't a comfortable ship plying between here and Belle Isle and I'm not having my wife tossed about in a banana boat. Third, as your friend says, Belle Isle is warmer —

and this is quite as warm as she can take. In fact, I was going to ask you about that place called North Point. It stands high and is cooler, I'm told. You could drive up there, have lunch at that . . . no, take a picnic." He remembered that it was at the place famous for its seafood that young Hamilton had had beer flung in his face. "A picnic and a lie-low and one of those big sun-shades," he said. "Then she can rest. It won't hurt you and Sarah to scramble down a cliff in order to bathe. But mind you — if you seriously think the guillotine will be back outside the cathedral on Easter Monday, I'm not holding you here."

Somewhere, in the back of Linda's mind there was an echo; London, the autumn chill and sludge in the streets, Mrs. Gordon saying, "My husband is a practicing optimist . . ."

8

THE picnic at North Point was a great success. "It was a breath of real fresh air and it *is* different from air conditioning," Mrs. Gordon said. "I feel restored, ready for Mr. Parker's dinner party. At least, as far as one could ever be. I know he means well but he *is* pompous and I do find him a bit wearing."

"I find him worse — quite embarrassing," Linda said. "All those orchids." And his seating her, the only unmarried woman, on his right; giving her precedence over the rest, all older, all married.

She maneuvered the Seagull down the road, all hairpin bends until they reached level ground at the turn off, Santa Barbara on the right, Caterina on the left.

"I don't feel very well," Sarah said, alighting from the car.

"Darling, what is it? In what way don't you feel well?" Mrs. Gordon asked anxiously.

"I just feel shaky and shivery. I don't feel well enough to be left with Theresa or go across to the MacNamaras and be left with Ian and his dog."

Linda said, "If you feel shivery I'd better take your temperature." Sarah had eaten about two-thirds of the picnic, sprawled on the pinkish sand, swum in the blue, tepid water, collected a lot of sea-shells, seemed in the best of health and spirits.

But the thermometer, under Linda's slightly cynical eye registered one hundred and one degrees. Poor child, she must be feeling extremely unwell — and I thought she was foxing!

"Sarah, hop into bed. I'll go and ask your mother to ring Mr. Parker and say I shan't be coming. It'll come better from her. And then I'll ring Ian and say you won't be going. And I think perhaps Dr. MacNamara should look in on you, on his way to the party. You have a little temperature."

"Not enough to make a fuss about. I feel a bit better now I'm in bed."

"Still it would do no harm," Linda said.

Sarah said, "Excuse me, I must just go to the bathroom." Dr. MacNamara, unusually spruce in his dinner jacket, with which he wore the old-fashioned, stiff-collared, stiff-fronted shirt, waited and then took her temperature himself because he had learned from bitter experience that to women one hundred point five read as one hundred and five.

Sarah's read one hundred and seven when she came back from the bathroom holding a mouthful of hot water. And that was impossible, he knew. People with temperatures of one hundred and seven didn't skip out of bed and into bathrooms and back again. It was his sight, a bit tricky lately. He certainly needed glasses. The beginning of the end! And like all things, a bit sudden. This little warning sign and another, ignored, and then *smack*!

He shook down the thermometer and without giving a sign of the smack he had just received said, "Keep her quiet. Light diet. And a couple of aspirins would do no harm."

"So now we're all happy," Sarah said. "You didn't really want to go, did you?

We'll have a nice quiet evening. Would you like to play Scrabble? Oh, brother! There's the telephone. Answer it in Mummy's room."

"Cables and Telegrams," the voice said. "Caterina 24? I have a cable. Ransom? It is from Felixstowe, England. It says *Aunt Edna dying — asking for you — come at once Mary*. Confirmation will be sent by the next post. Okay?"

"Yes, thank you," Linda said, feeling, despite all Mr. Gordon's assurances, very slightly sick.

"Excuse me," the voice said. "If you wish to send an answer, I will take it now." Helen's friend. And very thorough.

"There is no answer," she said.

* * *

What Helen — and perhaps Isabel — had expected did not happen. The only disturbance in Port Philip, indeed in the whole of the island, was very minor and nothing new. The faithful Catholic majority held the usual Easter processions and in two places a few people, atheistically inclined, jeered. In one place no notice was taken; in the other a banner-bearer hit the jeerer with the pole, the jeerer retaliated. The police, never far away, arrested them both and on Monday morning a magistrate who was equally impartial fined them both five dollars.

During the following week the Gordons themselves gave a dinner party which included Mr. Parker, who observed two things with disapproval; one that little English girls of ten were allowed to stay up for dinner and second that Angus Hamilton, "the pig doctor" as he scornfully thought of him, was regarded almost as a member of the family.

In his own curiously involved way, Mr. Parker had already paid Linda marked attention. On the very day of her arrival he had invited her to dinner with her employers! She had not been able to accept. Then he had come to dinner with the Gordons and had been extremely civil to her, behaving as though she were the daughter of the house. And next day when, in the traditional manner, he sent flowers to his hostess of the previous evening, he also sent flowers to Miss Ransom. At the president's reception he had looked out for her, meaning to show her singular favor again, but he had somehow missed her until the moment when she was leaving. Then, in a few spluttering compliments he had tried to make up for lost time. He had then asked if she would care to join the Bach Society and that was an honor indeed. She had thanked him, very prettily, but said that she was not musical. Then he had invited her to his rather special pre-Easter dinner and, defying all protocol, had arranged for her to take precedence, in the table seating, of several married ladies. The horrible child had fallen ill and at the last moment Miss Ransom had cancelled. And the infuriating thing was that nobody, save Mr. Parker himself, seemed to realize what was afoot.

The truth was that all English people were stupid. Heads of solid bone. They learned various tricks — but so did monkeys. Englishmen who had learned their tricks properly could be hired — as Mr. Gordon was, and Mr. Wilson, the electric expert, Dr. MacNamara, a score more. Despising the English as he did, and yet proud of his father's English name, why did Mr. Parker desire to marry an English wife ?

Mr. Parker asked himself that question often enough — by day when, insisting upon the trivia of routine, he drove Mr. Gordon almost mad, and in the night when the question was even more confused.

Mr. Parker could give himself several answers. And they varied. An English wife would have no relatives. What the English did with their dependents nobody exactly knew, but what was plain, and had been for years, was that they did not drag them about after them, an ever-lengthening chain — my brother, my brother-in-law, my cousin, nephew . . . even Nelson. Mr. Parker had little respect for Nelson, but it was a fact, he had read it. Nelson's stepson had served in the English navy and whenever he put a foot wrong had been slapped down, like anybody else. When you married an Englishwoman you were not instantly committed to eight, ten, a dozen other people. And if, today, you married an Englishwoman you were doing her a favor, being able to offer what no Englishman could, freedom from washing dishes, floors, shirts; any Englishwoman would be grateful for that. And there was also the past to be avenged. . . . That damned, bloody

English private soldier who had seduced a decent Spanish-Amerindian girl and then, pressed by her brothers, had gone into St. Sebastien's and said "I do." Since he had attained a little power Mr. Parker, very politely and adhering strictly to the rules, had pressed upon every English person with whom he came in contact. With an Englishwoman in his home, in his bed, opportunities would be endless. Muddled in with these motives was the fact that he admired Linda and thought her very attractive, partly because she was so typically English!

His difficulty was that even here, he had stuck to the rules. Private Parker, having bestowed his name and the army wife's allowance on his pretty brown sweetheart, had felt that his duty was fully discharged, so Mrs. Parker had returned to her family and her son had been brought up in the strict atmosphere of the island lower middle class where there were well-tried rules governing every aspect of behavior. The value of these rules was proved by what had happened to his mother who had ignored them and only just escaped ruin. Until that week after Easter, Mr. Parker had shown his preference — and his intentions — in a way any decent Santa Marian family would have understood; now he realized that he had been signaling to the blind and must change his tactics. But even now, though he was prepared to bend the rules a little, he would do it in an orthodox way. So he spoke first to Mr. Gordon, asking permission to take Miss Ransom out for an evening.

"But you asked me that once before," Mr. Gordon said, "when you wanted her to go with you to some musical affair. I told you then that Miss Ransom is a free agent and capable of arranging her own affairs."

Stupid! A monkey who had learned all about machinery.

"This is rather different, Mr. Gordon. At the Bach Society there would have been other people. I am now proposing to take Miss Ransom out for an evening — alone."

"Then she's the one to ask," Mr. Gordon said, anxious to end this talk. He saw quite enough of Mr. Parker at the factory; a civil exchange of hospitality was essential, but there was no need for them to go into a huddle, here, over such a trivial matter.

Mr. Parker wrapped his invitation up carefully. "I wondered, Miss Ransom, whether you had yet had an opportunity to visit your old home?"

"Nelson Bay?"

"It is called Carib Bay now."

"No. I mean to. In the daytime, when I drive, I usually take Mrs. Gordon in the North Point direction where it is slightly cooler. Nel . . . Carib Bay lies very low."

"I think you would be interested to see how greatly the place has improved. If you would allow me to take you there one evening, I should be delighted to show you around."

She answered a bit indirectly. "I rather wanted to go by day. To see my parents' grave — and the old house, and the place where I learned to swim. . . . "

"Ah," Mr. Parker said a trifle archly, "you are remembering the place as it was in the old days. It is now well-lighted, every inch of it. Even the beach, which is now a Lido. As for the house, I have no doubt that with me you could not only view it from the outside, you could go in. I am acquainted with the family who now occupy it. The exterior has not changed — it must not change, being one of the really old Spanish houses — but inside it, too, has vastly improved."

"I would like," Linda said rather drily, "to see how that kitchen could have been improved."

"Then you will come. When? I will suit myself to your convenience — and to that of Mr. and Mrs. Gordon, of course." He gave her this little reminder that she was, after all, an employed person and that in singling her out for attention he was paying her an enormous compliment.

"Tomorrow? Mr. and Mrs. Gordon, after this evening, will not be going out, I'm sure."

"Splendid," Mr. Parker said. His mind immediately busied itself with the idea of giving her an evening that she would never forget. He would not use his general issue Toledo, but the official black car!

"Well, well, well," Mr. Gordon said, when he saw it. "When I wanted the damned thing, that day when Sarah chopped her hair, I practically had to give a pint of blood! Have a nice time, my dear."

There was a poem, which Linda had once read with emotion, dealing with the difference between the outer manifestations of grief for the dead and remembering them. It comforted her now. It might sound callous to have been back in Santa Maria for something over three months and not have visited the place where her parents lay. But it had never seemed to be an errand of urgency. In her mind they lived, the father so conscientious and idealistic, the mother with her humor, on the caustic side. She remembered them. And, standing by their last physical resting place, brilliantly illuminated by the kind of floodlighting which she took for granted, but which had in fact been specially ordered, at very short notice by Mr. Parker, she thought, almost dispassionately that in a way they were lucky; they had worked together, and died together. Neither left, crippled by bereavement, to mend up a broken life. And neither of them would have cared for the changes which Mr. Parker was so complacent about. The little place, admittedly happy-go-lucky and a bit slovenly, had changed out of all recognition; industrialized; regimented. It had been a place of little, low huts, with chickens, pigs, goats and dogs at large, of little gardens. Children everywhere. And the beach had been a place where children splashed about and learned to swim — the rule being swim or drown — and the fishermen put out in their ancient boats.

Why it should seem so depressing she could not exactly say. There were blocks of flats — not dissimilar to the one in Port Philip where Angus lived. "Those who work must be properly housed," Mr. Parker said. Linda's father would have agreed with him; he had always held that the hovels were unhygienic. The new factories were not unsightly — the Toledo cars were made here and there was a huge canning factory; the fishermen were no longer dependent upon the day's sales. . . .

And there was the Lido, well-lighted, bright as day. "People who work by day must swim in the evening," Mr. Parker said; and there they were swimming, splashing, playing games on the pinkish sand, drinking beer, lime juice and Coca-Cola, eating fried potatoes and red hot banana fritters, served on little circles of fringed paper. All very much improved;

that nobody could deny. And why should anyone *wish* to deny it? Why should I? And why am I glad that I am here, with all these winds of change blowing about me, with somebody who thinks it is all marvelous? There was no clear answer to that; but she knew that had she returned with Mr. and Mrs. Gordon she would have felt obliged to say that the place in which she had been born and spent her childhood had been nicer then, more primitive, but nicer. Had she come with Angus she could have said, "I *loathe* it; it's like the North Circular Road on holiday at Blackpool." He would have understood.

"And now," Mr. Parker said, "we will go to your former home, and you shall see. . . . " Not only the improvements that had been made to the house, in which now lived the manager of the canning factory, but the respect, the near awe with which the manager and his wife behaved toward Mr. Parker.

Outwardly the house had changed little, though the garden was better kept: inside it had completely changed, with what had been the parlor and the dining room now thrown into one apartment, known as the lounge; the old kitchen had been made into a dining room, and a brand-new kitchen built, unit by unit into what had been her father's surgery. Here, far more than in the churchyard, memory sharpened. It was a mistake to have come, and she was glad that Mr. Parker refused an invitation to stay for dinner, an invitation extended very warmly. He had, he said, already bespoken a table at the Lido Restaurant. He said, "Another time, perhaps, if you will ask us . . . "

A girl far more inclined than Linda was to mistake mere civility for admiration might have been forgiven for not regarding Mr. Parker as an admirer. Until more than halfway through the meal his talk had been a resumption of the near monologue praising all things new which he had begun on that first drive. Linda realized why Mrs. Gordon found him tedious. "A lute with one string is a very poor thing." And such talk left one with so little to say except, "Yes indeed", "I see", and "That is so". For all that he said was true. The poverty in this area had been appalling. In the old days the people now happily disporting themselves in the arc-lit water would, if they went on to the beach at all, have been in search of driftwood or anything else the sea cared to throw up. They had lived in little hovels, cooked over outdoor fires, been ragged, been barefoot, uneducated.

"This," Mr. Parker said, including the whole of Carib Bay in the sweep of his hand, "is a very special project; government owned and still very much subsidized; new industries, like young children, must be supported. But, like the father of a family, the government can afford to support only so many. That is why, as you no doubt know, the wages at Santa Barbara tend to be low. The wage structure there was established in the old days. Men at the sugar mill earn twice, often three times what they did before, but they are still ill-paid by comparison. That is a situation which will mend itself. And it is this place, rather than North Point, with its old-fashioned nonsense, that should be the focus of tourist attention."

Suddenly she felt in full agreement with him. "I went there once — I mean into the seafood restaurant, and I thought it was all rather phoney. I mean I could look back and I never saw a . . . " she had been about to say "native girl" and that would have been disastrous, because Mr. Parker was one of the many native kinds. The trouble was there were so many of them; she was one; Helen Shawcross was one, Dolores Heredia y Heredia was one, and there were others . . . "waitress," she said, hitting on a happy compromise, "wearing so little, or carrying a tray on her head."

"Exactly," Mr. Parker said. "But tourists must be catered for. They bring in currency. And they go away and talk. They remember places where they had what they call a good time. One must be tolerant — for a time."

This section of the Lido restaurant was the most expensive, the least frequented, its lighting muted, the background music, raucous in other rooms, a mere murmur. A suitable place for man to take the next, necessary step. Mr. Parker said, "Miss Ransom, may I call you Linda? It is such a beautiful name. And this has been such a beautiful evening."

She said, "Why not. Everybody else does."

"My name is Francisco."

"Oh yes. That is a beautiful name, too. Of all the saints I always liked St. Francis best — he had a feeling for animals."

"Ah, yes. He preached, one is told, to the birds and addressed his donkey as *little brother*. I am not a Catholic."

"Oh, neither am I; but I think some of the stories about saints are charming. That St. Theresa, for example, who, when she fell from her mule in midstream said — 'God, if this is how You treat Your friends small wonder you have so few!'"

"Oh yes," Mr. Parker said, without interest. His dark face maintained its gravity.

"Linda," he said, "in asking permission to use your name, I was preparing the way. I have spoken to Mr. Gordon and he informs me that to the best of his knowledge you are not betrothed to anyone. Is he correct?"

"Quite correct." What next? Preparing the way for what?

"The next thing is *not* correct," he said ruefully, "but we have no parents to make the preliminaries for us. So may I suggest that we become betrothed?"

It was — as Victorian girls were trained to say, all so sudden! She had vision of herself saying, "But Mr. Parker, it is all so sudden!" That and his pomposity inspired an undignified impulse to giggle so that for a second or two she dared not attempt to speak. "The proposal should not be a complete surprise," Mr. Parker said, mistaking the reason for her silent stare. "You must have been aware of my admiration and interest, from the moment we met. I have since then conceived a deep respect for your character. My prospects are excellent. . . . " Here again he was forced to say for himself what in more orthodox circumstances would have been said for him. "I have sound reason to believe that I shall be the next minister of agriculture. As wife of a minister you would occupy a high position, and a very pleasant house in Port Philip." The linking of these two advantages was amusing too.

"You flatter me very much," she said, "but I am afraid that what you propose is impossible, Mr. Parker."

"Francisco."

"Francisco. Quite impossible."

"Why?"

Why? She was old-fashioned enough to think — Well, first because I do not love you. But love, she noted had not been mentioned. And imagine life spent alongside anyone so fundamentally egotistical, so lacking in humor, so given to monologue. Let alone the unfortunate affliction which Sarah had mentioned so rudely. None of this could be said, yet she must give some sort of answer, and it must be one that would not wound his self-esteem.

She said, "The truth is, I am not the marrying kind."

"What do you mean by that?"

"I'm too fickle. I never stay in the same mind about anything for more than about two months at a stretch. I never settle. I didn't settle in England. And to be honest, except for the fact that I gave my word to stay a year with the Gordons, I shouldn't be here now. I just happen to be one of those people for whom the grass is always greener on the other side of the fence."

"But marriage would cure that," Mr. Parker said gravely. "That you should not wish to stay with the Gordons is understandable. Acting in a menial capacity. Tied to that horrible child. I can assure you, married to me you would find life so easy and delightful, you would never wish to change."

I should be bored to death in a week!

She said, "No, I am sorry. It wouldn't work. I can see the advantage of a settled life, a home of my own, and a husband of splendid character and high position. But there would come a morning when I should see a liner — or even a banana boat — about to leave and I should just hop on it. I know myself, you see."

In the blend of blood that made Mr. Parker what he was there was a strong enough Catholic strain to make the thought of divorce repugnant to him; enough of Private Parker to make him feel that women should stay put, though men could move on; and enough, from some more ancient source to assure him that a man who couldn't hold a woman was a figure of ridicule. A wife, hopping on to a banana boat! He was capable of being sorry and at the same time thankful that she had refused him. But he said, with typical pomposity, "It is obvious to me that you do not love me."

A number of stinging answers sprang into her mind, but she remembered that he had, within his lights behaved correctly —

and that down in Santa Barbara Mr. Parker had the ability to make Mr. Gordon's life easier or harder. So she wished not to hurt his feelings, and not to anger him.

She said, "Ah, you see, Francisco, whether I do, whether I don't . . . and I do not propose to tell you . . . that is what I mean about knowing myself. Once, quite a long time ago, I was head over heels in love. It lasted exactly four months."

So lightly dismiss a searing experience, turn it to use. Forget being ditched by Charlie and all those tears in an autumn in Oldham, with the rain falling gray, from a gray sky onto a gray pavement.

"I think," Mr. Parker said, having given that statement some consideration, "that you may be a victim of circumstance. At home neither in Santa Maria, nor in England. And an orphan. I myself had a very stable background. . . . " True in a way. . .

Without rancor, armored in self-approval, he paid the bill and drove her home, the small defeat ignored, manners observed. Taking leave of him Linda said, "Thank you for arranging everything so beautifully. And I'm sorry about . . . "

"You were very honest with me," Mr. Parker said.

And that, Linda remembered afterwards, was Thursday.

9

IT was on the following Monday morning that Sarah said, "Miss Ransom, I don't want to argue, but what is the use? I am bad at figures. And you can buy little ready reckoners that tell you what simple interest should be. My grandmother in Scotland had one, even her milk bill; she could look it up. So why do we bother?"

Why indeed?

"Well there are things called examinations, Sarah. In order to get into school you must be prepared to face an examination and it might include a problem dealing with simple interest."

"Then I should write, 'Consult Reddish's Ready Reckoner.' I remember its name because it was so like radish."

"And you would fail."

"Well, *would* I?" Sarah asked seriously. "Don't you think that whoever had to mark all those sums might be glad to know about the Ready Reckoner? Or glad to see something different, just for a change? I know I would. And there is the telephone. Shall you or I . . . ?"

"You work out that sum," Linda said, and she went from the shady corner of the veranda where the lesson had been in progress and picked up the telephone. It was Angus. "Linda? Listen. Stay indoors for a couple of days. I can't . . . " The ordinary human voice gave way to a raucous roar. She said into the receiver, "Angus . . . can you hear me? Hullo, hullo, hullo . . . " The roar suddenly clicked into silence. She replaced the receiver and then picked it up again, waiting to give the operator his number and ask why, what did he mean? But it was dead, a bit of black plastic in her hand, connected with nothing. She tried three times, knowing that the telephone system was new, liable to failure. When she finally gave up and went out to the veranda, Mr. Gordon was there — ten o'clock in the morning. Saying to Sarah, "I never knew you were such a dunce, darling." Saying, "I have an unexpected holiday. Of course nobody bothered to tell me, but its a saint's day or something."

"Lovely," Sarah said. "You'll be able to come swimming with us."

"No fear!" Mr. Gordon said emphatically, "Catch me spending my holiday frizzling in the sun. We're all going to stay in this nice air-conditioned house for a couple of days . . . " Linda looked at him sharply; his voice, his face, his manner were controlled, his hands more than usually uneasy. ". . . and play canasta," he said.

"For money?"

"Sixpence a hundred if you like, you mercenary little monkey. Now, run up and tell Mummy about my holiday."

"What is it, Mr. Gordon?" Linda asked as soon as Sarah had gone.

"Nothing really. Nothing to worry about. There's some kind of demonstration down at Port Philip — votes for goats, or some such nonsense. But we had a telephone call warning us all to stay indoors or at least in Caterina for a couple of days."

"I had one, too. It was Angus. But he was cut off and when I tried to call back the telephone seemed dead."

"Operators gone demonstrating! Don't look so worried, Linda. I can see the point of the warning. If a roughhouse breaks out — they're an excitable lot — and a foreigner happened to be around, well, you know. International incident. Headlines. What we have to remember is that we are foreigners here. And I don't want Juliet to worry. We had a nasty little experience once. In Peru. Not that there'll be anything like that *here*. Fernandez is far too stable. Ah, there you are, my dear. . . . "

"Daddy, do we play partners or singly?"

"Whichever you prefer."

"Singly then."

Mr. Gordon played very badly and at eleven o'clock said, "I think a holiday merits a drink. If you'd get some ice, Linda. I'll make you the best martini you ever had."

Linda went into the kitchen. At this hour Juan would ordinarily be just back from the Santa Barbara market with his bicycle laden, fresh meat, fish, fruit and vegetables and Theresa would be scolding about the quality or the size. Today the kitchen was deserted and not tidy. Even the breakfast things were not washed up; both the larder door and the door of the cupboard in which tinned and packaged goods were stored stood ajar. And in both the shelves were as bare as Mother Hubbard's. Crossing the kitchen, she opened the door of Theresa's room. It was completely stripped. The move had been long planned; that was obvious; things taken out of the house a few at a time. More sinister was the assumption that the theft could be committed with impunity; that it was safe to take even the bed linen.

Carefully, Linda closed all doors and went to the refrigerator. There was some ice in the freezing chamber, and nothing else at all. Not even a bottle of Sarah's Coca-Cola. How explain that? In front of Mrs. Gordon who must not be worried.

From some niche of memory came the story of the little Dutch boy who had attempted to stop a flood by holding his hand in the hole in the dyke. Her task was just as hopeless. Yet she returned to the living room and said in what she hoped was a gay, holiday voice, "I wondered if just for once Sarah could have a small glass of sweet vermouth, well-iced."

"Like Mummy's!" Sarah took to the idea with alacrity.

They all drank. Then Linda, thinking

how fortunate it was that Sarah should have elected to play singly, excused herself from the game. "I have a few things to do," she said, and slipped into the kitchen, out by the rear of the house and into the Mac-Namara's back yard. Through the screen door she could see movement in the kitchen and, except that Rufus was not there with his usual greeting, all seemed normal. But it was not Maria who stood at the kitchen table, it was Mrs. MacNamara, wearing a gay apron and rolling out pastry.

She looked at Linda with recognition and relief, and then behind her and seemed to suffer some disappointment.

"Oh," she said, "I hoped you'd got him."

"Who?"

"That damned dog. He's gone wandering off again. There must be a bitch on heat somewhere nearby, though I can't think of one. And he's twelve at the very least." She lifted the sheet of pastry over a pie plate and cut it around in two skillful movements.

"Where is Maria?"

"Oh, she asked for the day off — one of her many relatives is sick. And Luis is later back from market than I've ever known. Not that it matters, I'm well stocked up. I wouldn't bother with lunch but both my boys will be home. Ian got an unexpected holiday, so he's gone into Port Philip with his father. The hospital rang up, they wanted him to give the anesthetic for an emergency operation." She began to nick scallops around the edge of the pie. In the presence of her cheerful, matter-of-fact competence Linda's fears seemed grotesque.

"I've really come to borrow, Mrs. Mac."

Mrs. MacNamara was not surprised. She liked Juliet Gordon as a person, but thought poorly of her as a housekeeper. ("Please don't mention it to anyone," Mrs. Gordon had said, putting herself into Doctor MacNamara's care. "There's a sort of vulture quality; everybody waiting for you to die." So when Mrs. MacNamara said to her husband, in a certain voice and with a certain look in her eye, that Mrs. Gordon relied too much upon her hired help, and really should look into what was in that great basket Theresa took with her whenever she went out, Doctor Mac-

Namara said, "She's new here, remember," or even made such a nationalistic statement as, "After all, she's English.")

"Theresa has run away," Linda explained. "And she took with her everything movable. All our stores. The sheets from her own bed."

Mrs. MacNamara halted the knife. The freckles on her face were suddenly very prominent.

"When?" she asked, almost in a whisper.

"During the night — but she must have been moving things for days."

"My God! My boys!" She dropped the knife and still wearing the apron, dashed to the garage where stood the car which she had inherited when it was judged to be insufficiently reliable for her husband's use. She jabbed the self-starter which made a useless noise.

"Do you think. . . . ?"

"I know. It's just how . . . " the starter roared again. "You bloody, bloody . . . " said Mrs. MacNamara, who never swore. She jabbed again, the engine sprang to life. "Help yourself," she shouted as the old car leaped and almost stalled. "And be caaarefullll." She rocked away in a cloud of engine fumes. The last word trailed on the air.

* * *

In the sinisterly quiet house Linda found a basket and methodically collected food for two days from a cupboard and larder even better stocked than their own had been yesterday. The absence of Theresa and Juan could not be long concealed but the depredation might. It was at the mention of the stealing that Mrs. Mac had turned pale. Linda guessed that had she been able to hear the full sentence it would have ended, ". . . it started last time". The Macs had lived on the island for ten years.

Opening the living room door, she said, "I've made rather a makeshift lunch. Theresa and Juan appear to have taken French leave."

"How very inconsiderate," Mrs. Gordon said. "You shouldn't have done it all on your own, Linda. I could have helped and Sarah could have set the table." Fortunately Theresa had not taken the cutlery or the table silver — some of it old and good. Perhaps because it was in the dining room and she had forgotten it; perhaps because such things were traceable.

Without looking up from his cards, Mr. Gordon said, "I'll give them French leave! Run off to this d . . . saint's thing, of course."

"I'd like to see it, too," Sarah said. "Daddy couldn't we go down this afternoon. Do you remember that one in Austria?"

"This would be nothing like that, darling. That was a show piece for visitors; balcony seats reserved. This'll be just a noisy, smelly crowd and we should see nothing."

Linda went to his aid. "That is perfectly true, Sarah. I've seen several. All you see is a crowd, making an excuse to get drunk, just like a football crowd. You get your toes trodden on, and somebody is quite likely to be sick down your back."

"How loathesome!" Sarah said.

Mrs. Gordon said, "Linda, please! We're just about to have lunch."

When the lunch was eaten Mr. Gordon jumped up busily.

"Now I will wash up. Darling you go to lie down . . . no, I insist. . . . But of course,

I suppose the beds . . . Sarah you go and make Mummy's bed, never mind about mine . . . and your own. I'll wash and Linda'll wipe. After all," he said sturdily, "We're only living for a short time the way people in England live all the time."

In the kitchen he said, "Now, Linda. When did you know they'd gone?"

"When I fetched the ice. The point is, obviously they don't intend to come back. Between them they stripped the larder, the store cupboard and the refrigerator. I had to go and borrow . . . " She told him of her borrowing visit to Mrs. Mac and of Mrs. Mac's reaction.

"So long as she doesn't know," he said, jerking his head upward and sideways toward the conjugal bedroom. He removed his linen jacket and rolled up his shirt-sleeves. "And personally I see no reason to panic. There may be a bit of a rumpus. I suppose the left hand lot will go on promising people like Theresa immunity and plenty forever; and the right hand lot promise to restore the lost acres. . . . " He washed two plates thoughtfully. "I must say I did not foresee . . . I was offered a job with the British Sugar Corporation, but it meant living in Peterborough where you'd be damned lucky to get a woman one half day a week. And that wasn't what I wanted for her." He washed another plate. "You've been a wonderful girl, Linda; I'm very grateful. And don't you go getting worried. Nothing's going to happen to us; far too valuable . . . " Encouraged by that thought, he said, "Make a list of what we need, Linda, and I'll run down to Santa Barbara and stock up."

"But you were told to stay here."

"Not without food."

"Please don't risk it, Mr. Gordon. Two separate people have told me that last time there was fighting in the street — quite serious. I can go on borrowing."

"She might notice that. Then she'd have to know and then she would be scared. You see," he said, slowly wiping his hands and pulling down his sleeves, "that time in Peru — we lived in a great pink palace and had a dozen servants and the first sign of trouble was their running off with everything they could carry. Come on, buck up with that list, I must get there and back before she's about again." All the genuine cheer and the false, too, had deserted him now, and he looked what he was, a troubled man.

"Just think," Linda said, "what would happen to her, if anything happened to you. I won't let you go. I shall simply scream for Mrs. Gordon to come down and stop you herself. Honestly, I mean that. To save her a little scare would you make a widow of her?" He blenched.

"You're right, of course."

"I'll pick my time and slip across to the Mac's again."

Sarah had timed it, she thought, precisely. She had made her mother's bed with meticulous care; her own rather roughly; then, judging that the washing up would be done, sauntered into the kitchen.

"What are we going to do this afternoon, Daddy?"

"Go and visit Mr. Parker," Mr. Gordon said after an almost imperceptible hesitation. "You missed your swim in the sea — but you could have one in his pool. And then when it is cooler play tennis."

Mr. Parker's house had amenities that the other houses in Caterina lacked.

"Well, better than nothing, I suppose," Sarah said grudgingly.

"We'll wait till Mummy gets up," Mr. Gordon said.

"Could we make a picnic there? I absolute hate it when he holds a plate of sandwiches and spits."

"That is a marvelous idea, Sarah. Mr. Parker may not be at home." He was not. Indeed it had been Mr. Parker, telephoning from Port Philip who had warned Mr. Gordon to go home and stay there for two days.

"Good," Sarah said. "We'll make a picnic." The difficult, arbitrary thing which lay side by side with simple childishness, retreated. She was a child, natural, in her proper age group as she said, "What shall we have, Linda?" and turned toward the almost empty cupboard which yawned emptily behind what Linda had snatched up from Mrs. Mac's.

"I'll get it," Linda said. "You couldn't reach." It occurred to her that perhaps it would have been better to take Sarah into their confidence; explain. And it may come to that, she thought. But she opened the door of the store cupboard as little as possible and pretended to reach up and hand down a tin of salmon. The can opener was fixed to the wall and had escaped Theresa's attention. "Open it, Sarah, you know how it works. And mash it into paste. I'll cut the bread and butter."

"How about Ian?" Sarah asked, mashing vigorously. "With his dog he is a bore, but Mr. Parker won't have the thing in and Ian without Rufus is *almost* human."

"Are they home?" She had herself looked out twice; Doctor MacNamara's fairly new Toledo, gray, always stood in front of the house, ready, aye ready! He could not be bothered with garage doors and very soon his new car would be as neglected looking as the one in which Mrs. MacNamara had jolted away.

"No," Sarah said. "Not a sign of life. A pity!"

"I rather think," Linda said, "that they may be taking advantage of the holiday. Doctors don't get many and Doctor Mac-Namara does love to go fishing."

"So there we are," Sarah said, accepting the situation and proffering the well-mashed salmon. "Now, what about the tea?" The picnics at North Point had always included a thermos jug of tea.

Mr. Gordon had busied himself at the

sink, lifting his head at the mention of his neighbor, lowering it again, waiting, listening. "Where's the thermos jug?" Sarah asked, "It always stood . . ."

It always stood, blue and bulging on one of the built-in shelves, the modern version of a dresser, alongside the kitchen clock and an egg timer. Theresa had evidently thought it worth taking.

"We don't need tea, Sarah," he said. "If Mr. Parker's old crone is there, she'll make it for us. If she's gone holidaying like the rest of them, you or Linda can come back and make a pot of tea and bring it across. It isn't a mile away." His voice was edgy. Sarah put her head on one side and regarded him judicially.

"I don't think holidays really suit you."

* * *

Mr. Parker's house was occupied, though he himself was not at home. Rosa and three or four people, all bearing a strong family likeness were just finishing a meal of roast pork. Rosa said she would gladly make tea for them at whatever time they liked and deplored the fact that they had brought sandwiches. Mr. Parker, she said, had gone to Port Philip on Sunday and had not told her when he would be back.

Halfway to the pool Mr. Gordon stopped and said, "I've a good mind to ask her . . . she hasn't gone galloping off." He turned and went back to the kitchen, where as before, the chatter and laughter ceased abruptly, and five pairs of dark, lustrous eyes regarded him with interest.

"You want that tea now, sir," Rosa asked, heaving herself up.

"No. No thank you. It was just . . . well, our help has left us, rather unexpectedly. I wondered if any of you knew somebody who'd be willing to lend us a hand."

They all looked embarrassed. Mr. Gordon thought he had put the question as delicately as he could, accustomed as he was to the England where anybody doing a job in a house was obliging, doing a positive favor. Then Rosa said, "*You* could, Bella. After Wednesday." She was addressing what looked to be her twin sister.

"Would it be live-in, sir?"

"I should prefer that. But of course . . . well anything would be better than nothing. For the time being."

"Oh. I'd live in. After Wednesday."

With each mention of the specific day, something emanated from the group; very difficult to define, but Mr. Gordon expressed his thanks, his appreciation, his hope that Bella would be happy with them, and was left with the impression that the day was of importance to them as a group. Some family festival; perhaps even a member of the family expecting to be confined.

Walking, not ill-pleased with himself, toward the pool, he heard the laughter break out again. On a different note? Mocking? Mustn't get fanciful, he said to himself, and walked on.

Mrs. Gordon lay in a long chair and watched while the others swam in the pool. Then they had tea and played a half-hearted game of tennis. At this season it was still too hot for vigorous exercise, even after tea. Soon they all piled into the car — Mr. Gordon would not allow his wife to walk even that short distance — and went home.

"I've got a new woman," he said. "A good, solid creature, a relative of Rosa."

Immediately, he was in difficulties.

"Don't you expect Theresa back?"

"I wouldn't have her back. Walking off like that and leaving us in such a muddle. And not a word."

"I always hated Theresa," Sarah contributed.

Back in the house Mrs. Gordon said, "Now Linda, you've been exerting yourself all afternoon. I will make supper. I can cook, you may be surprised to hear."

Both Mr. Gordon and Linda thought of the empty shelves.

"We don't want a cooked supper," he said.

Linda said, "I thought not either. It's a kind of cold snack. And I left it practically ready; so there's absolutely no need for you to bother, Mrs. Gordon."

"You see," Mr. Gordon said. "You come and sit down and have a tiny drink and we'll see if the radio is working."

"I'm going to wash my hair," Sarah said. "That pool water is sticky. I expect he spits in it."

It seemed a favorable moment to slip across to the MacNamara's, borrow, if they were back, if not simply to take a few more stores so that should Mrs. Gordon, by some mischance, make her way into the kitchen, the truth might not be so obvious.

The brief twilight of the tropics had begun; the west was ablaze. Indoors one already needed a light, but there was none in the MacNamara's house — at least at the rear. They might be in their living room. And anyway, Linda thought, approaching the back veranda, Rufus had come home and he was not behaving like a dog who had returned to an empty house. He lay in his usual position, between the top of the veranda steps and the kitchen door; and in his usual posture, flat out on his side. He did not move as she approached and stepping level with him she spoke his name, looking down, waiting for, at least, a movement of the feathered, usually eager tail. Then with a draining away of heart, breath, viscera into an unfathomable hollow, and only the mind alert, in place and vulnerable, she saw that the dog was dead and that attached to his collar was a label, so soiled as not to stand out, white, between his red-brown hide and the veranda floor. In big, black, block letters the message was legible even in the fading light. It read, "Forrin dogs not wanted hear."

A friendly, harmless old dog! Who could have been so cruel? So wicked? She saw the piece of rough rope which had choked life out of him. And as she stood there, shocked, two other emotions assailed her. Protectiveness; the realization of the need to conceal because one of those who must be protected — and she included Mr. Gordon — might so easily say — "I'll just step across and see if the Macs . . . " and so stumble, as she had stumbled, across this obscene evidence of hatred.

The Macs back yard, like the back yards of all the Caterina houses, was bordered at its farthest end by secondary jungle growth. More space had been cleared than had been used; the great trees had been torn out by the roots or sawed off at ground level before the houses had been built and the gardens made; in the space between the real jungle and the cultivated land, frailer growths had taken advantage of light and elbow room and sprung up, ebullient; small trees, bushes, flowering plants, creepers. Not dense, but seeming so, a ten-or twelve-foot-high hedge of varying greens, flowers of pink and white, purple, scarlet, yellow.

A hiding place. Once there, little predatory animals, flesh-eating birds, would reduce Rufus to a few unidentifiable bones in no time at all.

But the other emotion was fear. The light was fading and somewhere, in the gathering dusk, whoever had placed the dog and the unequivocal message here might be watching, waiting to see. . . .

She was not naturally a nervous person. Like most children she had, between the ages of four and five, suffered imaginary terrors; had disliked going upstairs when everybody else was on the ground floor, imagined wild beasts or malevolent witches in any unlighted corner. But she had been fortunate in her parents, who were never derisive, always rational, and such fears were soon outgrown. But now, standing on the veranda of the deserted house, the dead dog at her feet, she began to tremble; to be almost sure that somewhere hostile eyes were watching. Still the thing must be done, and there was no one else to do it. She lifted the dog, not easily — he seemed to weigh far more than he had done when alive — and carried him toward the jungle edge, shouldered her way in and laid him down. Then her courage was spent. She had done the essential thing and no amount of reasoning or will power could make her remount the veranda steps and go into the kitchen. For one thing, it was almost dark. Surely, never had darkness fallen quite so swiftly. To get what she needed from Mrs. Mac's store she would be obliged to put on the light and stand exposed to the watchful eyes. She thought dismally that Mr. Gordon's remark about being valuable did not apply to her. She was merely the foreign governess to a foreign child; as expendable as the dog. She began to run toward the lighted windows of the next-door house.

10

"NOT so much as a squeak," Mr. Gordon said, eyeing the radio with disfavour.

Mrs. Gordon remembered the incident in Peru. First the servants had disappeared; then telephone and radio had failed; then the electricity had been cut off. Ever since then, wherever she was she had made certain of having a supply of candles in the house. She thought now of candles, but said nothing. George worried if she worried.

"I'll just see how Sarah . . ." she said, deliberately vague, and went into the hall; but instead of going upstairs she crossed to the dining room which had a door communicating with the kitchen. She switched on the light and went to the store cupboard and knew the truth. Peru all over again!

She stood there for a moment and then, calmly went upstairs to see how Sarah was getting on with her shampoo. They must not know that she knew. They must be allowed the tiny satisfaction of thinking that they had successfully deceived her. For as long as possible. She thought it would not be long.

* * *

After supper the Wilsons came in and for once Mr. Gordon did not show any great pleasure at the sight of them. They might let slip an incautious word. And Mr. Wilson soon did, using the word demonstration.

"And what's your opinion, Gordon, about this damn fool demonstration?"

"Sound proof of how solidly Catholic the country really is," Mr. Gordon said in a quick, trenchant voice.

"Catholic?" Mr. Wilson said, looking amazed. Was the man off his head? The very reverse was true; this affair was Communist inspired.

"Surely, when a saint's day and a religious procession bring everything to a standstill and give even old heathens like us a holiday, it's proof of strong Catholic feeling."

"But . . ." Mrs. Wilson began, and then

was aware that Linda, beside whom she sat on the sofa, was pushing a sharp, warning elbow against her own well-padded one. "They don't act very Catholic," she finished weakly.

"Now that you've come," Mrs. Gordon said smoothly, "how about a game of bridge? Sarah, dear, would you like to run up and get those lovely new cards you gave me for Christmas." Sarah went and when she had been absent for half a minute, Mrs. Gordon said, "I doubt whether she'll find them. I'll just call up the stairs."

She went out into the hall, carefully closing the door behind her. Now the four who were in the know could get the thing straight between themselves.

* * *

"My wife's not to know. Get that? She's not very strong. I won't have her worried. Linda here and I have managed all day. . . . Help run off, having robbed us blind. But she's not to know."

"I see. I rather doubt whether you . . . Never mind. What do you think the outcome will be?"

"I don't know and I don't bloody well care, so long as they leave us alone; as they will. Whichever lot come out on top they'll want the factory kept going. I don't know about your contract, mine's with the *government* of Santa Maria and I don't give a damn what government that is. Come to that they could all kill each other and I shouldn't care. Best thing that could happen to fanatics."

"Now," Mrs. Gordon said, reentering, "shall we invite Sarah into this game. Darling, you're so good at canasta. Would you like to learn bridge? You could sit with me and I'd explain."

"I really think," Sarah said, "I've had enough for one day. Simple interest in the morning; then a new stroke at swimming and how to lob this afternoon."

Ungrateful, ungracious child, thought both the Wilsons, childless themselves. Even Ian MacNamara, a better handled child than most, was difficult about his old dog. As for Sarah Gordon? Spoiled rotten and saucy. There'd be trouble storing up there. Think of her at seventeen!

"Two hearts," Mr. Wilson said and the

game, a refuge, almost a kind of drug, had begun.

* * *

"And the evening and the morning were the first day." That was Monday. Tuesday was a repetition of it except that they all lunched with the Wilsons, whose refrigerator had not been robbed and whose help — an elderly married couple, sound Methodists — were not involved in either Catholic or Communist demonstrations.

Cooked for by them, waited upon by them, Linda remembered that Wesley, the founder of Methodism, was said to have saved England from revolution.

Mrs. Wilson had framed the invitation tactfully. "I ordered a leg of lamb," she said. "I have seen many legs of lamb but never one like this. Huge. Unless you come and help us out, Tom and I shall be eating cold mutton for a week."

She was tactful, too, about her other little offering. Could they use a few eggs? She'd ordered as usual on Saturday and then on Sunday a friend who kept fowls had called and brought her a dozen. Mrs. Gordon had always thought that except at the bridge table Mrs. Wilson was a bit of a bore; she now had one of her swift pangs of remorse and upon leaving, kissed Mrs. Wilson who was both surprised and flattered. In the hierarchy of the factory the manager ranked above the electrical engineer and Mrs. Wilson had always felt that though Mr. Gordon — sensible man that he was — was prepared to overlook this fact, Mrs. Gordon hadn't *quite*, and only associated with her because she played such a good game of bridge.

* * *

Shortly before six Mr. Gordon tried his radio again, and this time was rewarded. ". . . your neighbors, please?" a mechanical voice said. "I will repeat that. We apologize for the breakdown. Normal service is now resumed. Stand by for an important announcement at seven o'clock. Will those of you now listening try by telephone, or other means, to convey this information to your neighbours, please?" After the same slight pause it began again, "I will repeat that . . ."

"Only too gladly I will," Mr. Gordon said, moving to the telephone. The Wilsons and two other families had heard; several had not. One, the headmaster of the school in Santa Barbara which Ian MacNamara attended, let slip the information that he and his sister were only that moment back home, having been away for a long weekend. Yet Ian's holiday on Monday had been unexpected.

"I think I'll try Parker," Mr. Gordon said. "Darling, you didn't get your rest after lunch; don't you think you should lie down, just for half an hour. I'll call you for the announcement, of course." The suggestion was made with a casualness, slightly overdone.

"An excellent idea," she said and went away.

Mr. Gordon gave the number of the Sugar Administrative Office, above which there was a flat, Mr. Parker's pied-à-terre in Port Philip. The call was successful and quite lengthy. At its end Mr. Gordon went into the kitchen where Linda was. He said. "I've just talked to Parker. He was very cagey and told me nothing much; but he did ask me, *he* actually asked *me*, if I could run the factory without him. He was kind enough to say that if I could, and if I did, I *might* be left in sole charge. Think of that!"

"And what did you say?"

"If I'd said what was in my mind the telephone'd been out of action again. I said I'd do my best to struggle along."

"Good. I rather think Mr. Parker is about to be minister of agriculture."

"Oh, my good God, no! Ignorant, interfering, bumptious . . . Anyway, what makes you say that?"

"I have flashes of second sight."

"No, but seriously, Linda, it's no subject for joking. And it's just possible, too possible to be funny."

"Well, strictly between ourselves, Mr. Parker once hinted to me that it was not only possible, but likely. And it is good news, in a way. It indicates that whatever has been going on it has involved no *major* change."

"That's very true. Well, thank God it seems to be over."

"Yes, whatever it was. I think I'll ring Angus. He might be more informative." As she spoke the telephone rang. Mr. Gordon hurried to it, called, "It's for you. It's him."

"Hullo, Angus."

"Hullo, Linda. You all right?"

"Quite all right. And you?"

"Fine. Just back from Almerina — Pig Island, you know. Are you mad with me?"

"Should I be?"

"Well, we had that date for Monday and while I was trying to explain we were cut off. And I had no time to call back. I just hoped you'd understand."

"I did. I do," she said, understanding very little.

"I wondered about tomorrow, Wednesday. I'll be free then. I know how anxious you are to make this trip." What trip?

"I was, rather."

"Then I'll come. Six o'clock say?"

"That would suit me well."

"Till then."

*   *   *

"Did he tell you anything about what has been going on?" asked Mr. Gordon, who had tactfully absented himself.

"Not a thing. I don't think he knew much. He's been in Almerina — you know, that island devoted to keeping pigs in ideal conditions."

"And there again, you see. If what you say about Parker should be true . . . He once said to me that he thought it was a waste. He'd read somewhere — all his information was secondhand — that pigs on free range didn't gain weight quickly enough. He was all for caging them, with only just enough room to stand up or lie down. And maybe where sheer fat is the objective, he could have a point. I like my bacon lean, and if possible off a *happy* pig. They like *rooting* you know. Even ringing their noses was a defiance of nature, as well as a barbarity."

Such uncomfortable — and irrelevant — thoughts must be thrust aside. "Come along," Mr. Gordon said, "it's getting on for seven, when we shall be told all."

11

THERE was first the playing of the Santa Maria national anthem, a most adaptable piece of music. It had a calypso rhythm for cheerful occasions, another capable of switching over to stateliness when stateliness was required, and a third to match itself to the measured tread of marching men. Tonight it had a solemn boom and a break, too sad for words. It said, "All men must die". Into the new houses, and the old, into happy homes and unhappy ones, into those where the young lived, quieting their children, and into those where the old lived — those who had missed the radio most — the somber message made entrance and made also what followed not a surprise but the continuance, a fulfillment of what the music foretold.

Then a voice — unfamiliar — said gravely, "It is with the greatest possible regret and the most profound sorrow that I tell you that President Fernandez is dead."

There was a short, dramatic pause. Then the voice said, heart speaking to heart, "May I ask you, whoever you are, wherever you are, whatever you may be doing, to stand for a moment in silence as a tribute to the simple soldier who made Santa Maria independent, prosperous and peaceful. . . ."

Mr. Gordon said, "Don't you move, my dear." But he got to his feet himself, saying, "He was the best of them, so far as I could see."

Linda stood up too. Because Dolores had said, "But he was kind. Gentle . . ."

Sarah stood because they did and the solemn measure of the national anthem put an end to their rather awkward and self-conscious postures.

Seated again they heard the kindly, explanatory voice, speaking from the heart, telling them all. The president's death was a shock and a surprise to all but those most closely associated with him; only a few people knew that for some time his health had been a cause of concern. It was his own wish that his condition should be concealed; he wished to die in harness and he had insisted upon working until the very end. He was, as most people would remember, a soldier. General Fernandez before he was President Fernandez. And as a soldier he had died, at his post.

That voice ceased. Another took over, in a lighter, less emotional tone giving a rundown of Fernandez' career and achievements, and aims — to preserve Santa Maria as an independent, viable entity, a neutral in a world increasingly inclined to take sides. A man of the kind most needed in the world at this moment. Dedicated to his country and uncommitted to any faction or to any outside interest. It was no exaggeration to say that all over Santa Maria tonight the ordinary people would feel that they had lost a friend, one might almost say, a father.

That voice, having begun lightly, ended on an emotional note, too. One could imagine the speaker turning away from the microphone, stiffening his face, blinking his eyes against the threat of unmanly tears.

Then a third voice, heavier and even more solemn than the one that had announced the death, took up the tale.

That small circle of friends and colleagues who had been in the late president's confidence had known for some months not only that the president's health was failing, but that he wished Mr. Lopez, minister of education, to succeed him, to carry on his work and to pursue his aims. Many listening at the moment knew, through their own experience, and even more knew through their children, of Mr. Lopez' scope and vision and unstinting work in the field of education. That scope, that vision, those unstinting efforts would now be applied to the interests of the country as a whole. The welfare of Santa Maria and its people had been bequeathed by President Fernandez to Mr. Lopez, a legacy and a charge. . . .

"The news will be broadcast at nine o'clock, as usual."

"Well, well," Mr. Gordon said, turning off yet another rendering of the national anthem.

"One curious thing I noticed," Mrs. Gordon said, "nobody mentioned when Fernandez died. Or what ailed him."

Linda said, "I wonder if Dolores knew. If not, this will be a shock to her. Theirs wasn't a love match, but I think he had endeared himself to her, in a way."

Both Gordons made little sympathetic sounds.

"I wonder," Mr. Gordon said, "how the army's going to take this. Fernandez' was a military coup; it's been a military dictatorship. Are the soldiers going to take kindly to a desk-wallah?"

"I should imagine Fernandez would have considered that before bequeathing that legacy," Mrs. Gordon said. Mr. Gordon gave his wife a glance both sharp and appreciative. She seldom showed much interest in things outside her immediate orbit, but every now and again she was capable of making a dry, shrewd comment, very much to the point.

"Now will begin," he said, "a game of musical chairs. Everybody move one up. I may be left in sole charge of the factory yet!" When and if he did, Mrs. Gordon knew, it would cease to be *the* factory and become *my* factory. "We'll drink to the chance, anyway," he said.

* * *

The news at nine repeated, but still without detail, the news of Fernandez' death and, without eulogy, the news of Mr. Lopez' succession. But by some trick of phrasing both events were made to sound as though they had taken place some time ago. Fernandez was to be buried with full military honors on Thursday. All hearts would go out to his widow, prostrate with grief. It was hoped, but not yet certain, that she would be able to attend the funeral.

It was with regret that the announcer reported that this year, at a moment when the need for unity was most urgent, disturbances had broken out during the procession of St. Catherine of Cappodocia. Both sides had shown bigotry and become violent, so that police action was necessary. There had been some casualties and a number of arrests had been made. Such demonstrations were out of place in a modern country in the twentieth century and it was sincerely to be hoped that under the shadow of a common grief and in the light of an ever brightening future, all such differences and all old grievences would be put away.

Mr. Gordon reflected with satisfaction that it was over, whatever it had been.

The mere fact that the death and the succession had been announced indicated a certain stability. His experience was pretty varied and he had once been — thank God in a climate too torrid for Juliet to be with him — in a country so disturbed that when its ruler died his body had lain, rotting inside a metal-lined casket for a fortnight while in a nearby room, men, all of them in imminent danger of death themselves, argued out what was to be done, what said.

Mrs. Gordon made another of her comments. "The voices were different; but the speeches and the announcements, I'll swear, were all written, or dictated, by the same hand or mouth. Like poetry — once your ear is tuned in, you know, without looking, whether it's Shelly or Milton."

"I agree," Linda said. "And I'd say it's Mr. Lopez' voice. He spoke, if you remember, on my official visit to the hospital. There's the same *ring*."

"Very glib and rather evasive," Mrs. Gordon said. "I noticed at the time. And I thought how extremely suitable in a minister of education."

"The great thing is, business as usual tomorrow. And without Parker breathing down my neck."

12

SO now it was Wednesday. It began well. All of a sudden Sarah, abandoning thoughts of Reddish's Ready Reckoner, mastered the principles of simple interest and worked out six imaginary investments without fault.

Then a boy, skinny but wiry-looking, arrived on a bicycle even more decrepit than Juan's and said that his aunt Tessa was coming to work here tomorrow and he would rather like to work here, too. He'd begin tomorrow, but if the lady wanted anything today, this morning, he'd ride down to Santa Barbara and fetch it. Linda gave him the list she had denied Mr. Gordon. His name, he said was Miguel and either he was a better marketer than Juan or things were cheap that morning. He actually brought back some change, as well as everything required.

Mrs. Wilson, unaware of this improvement in the Gordon household, rang up and invited the female members of it to tea. Lunch on two consecutive days, would, she felt, be rather obvious; but she had planned a substantial tea.

Linda, planning to do a little washing, excused herself from this outing, but drove Mrs. Gordon and Sarah along at about half-past three; then, back, alone in the house, she set to work.

The kitchen window, under which the sink stood, overlooked an enclosure; to the left the garage wall, to the right the jut of the dining room, and straight ahead the wall of jungle growth. Neither wall actually reached to the trees and shrubs; between garage and jungle was the pathway that formed the back entrance to the house; between dining room and jungle was the path that led to the garden and so to the MacNamara's.

She was washing away, her thoughts running along pleasant lines. The crisis, whatever it had been, was over, no great damage done; proper help in the house tomorrow; and this evening she was going out with Angus to whom she would be able to speak openly of the trials and subterfuges of the last few days, when suddenly she had a return of the feeling she had experienced while standing by the dead dog. Somebody watching.

Nothing stirred anywhere; the somnolent silence hung so heavily that she could hear, as she stood listening, the minute sounds of the foam on the water.

She told herself, fanciful nonsense, the result of a hateful experience, contributed to, probably, by the empty house behind her, the empty house next door.

She went on washing, rinsed, wrung out; and then knew an aversion to the thought of going out to hang the things on the line that stretched across the yard, from a point near the kitchen door, to a point halfway along the wall of the garage.

"Forrin dogs not wanted hear." Foreign specialists in varying trades accepted so long as they were useful. Do I over-estimate my own importance when I think that someone might be bothering to watch me? Perhaps I do.

In the MacNamara's garden she had stayed long enough to drag the dog out of sight because that was a job that must be done. Over hanging out washing there was no such compulsion. She could leave the wet things where they lay, walk out of the house by the front door and get into the waiting Seagull — and ever after be a little bit ashamed of giving way to an imaginary fear : think herself neurotic.

Amost angrily she snatched up the basket of clothes, the bag of linen pegs, and went out, so placing herself that as she pegged she could see the two entrances to the yard, and the jungle. The snaking fear, thus defied, did not decrease as it should. Second by second she became more convinced of being under observation.

She was nearing the end of the line when a voice said, "Linda." She jumped at the sound; but the fear vanished. "Don't give any sign. Walk over to the pink ginger bush."

Her immediate thought was that it was Helen. Helen using a cautious voice. She walked toward the pink-flowered bush.

"The servants must not see me," the voice said.

"There are no servants. I am alone in the house."

There was a stir, a rustling of leaves, a cracking of twigs, and literally out of the jungle from behind the flowery bush came

Dolores. In one look Linda took in the tattered remains of a satin and lace nightdress, one of the short waterproof capes issued to soldiers, a pair of clumping army boots.

"I was afraid I'd never . . ." Dolores said; and then, the need to gain her journey's end no longer operative, she pitched forward. Linda reached to break the fall and was herself overborne and ended on her knees on the concrete of the yard with Dolores' face in her lap.

Head between the knees, her father had always said. She struggled up and with a great effort rearranged the limp body so that it was in that position. Dolores was very slight, but in this state heavy and difficult to handle. The long, black hair of the head forced down between the knees was tangled and full of bits of leaf and twig and flower petals.

The good old cure was so long in taking effect that she had begun to doubt its efficacy in this case. Then the body beside which she crouched, saying — though she was not aware that she was speaking at all — "Dolores! Dolores!" over and over again, took on living substance.

Dolores said, "It's all right. I'm all right." The tangled head came up, the face, whiter than paper. The great, dark eyes lifted, and even essayed a look of reassurance. "It was just . . ." Dolores said. "I knew that if I could get here . . . Oh Linda. It was so horrible. And if they find me, they'll kill me." She began, shakily, to get to her feet. Linda rose and putting an arm around her, guided her into the house. Into Theresa's room, onto the nearest bed, where, lying flat, Dolores began to cry. "It was so horrible. I was so frightened. I never loved him, but he was considerate, in his way. But whoever it was, it would have been horrible."

Another thing Linda's father had said often was — a good cry never did anybody any harm. So she waited until the first bitter outburst had passed and then said, "I'll get you some coffee. I shan't be a minute it only needs heating up."

"I've been drinking filthy water — what I could scoop up in my hand."

Linda plugged in the percolator, then, from the sitting room fetched the rum bottle and, as an afterthought, the cigarettes.

Dolores, calmer now, drank the well-laced brew avidly, and accepted a cigarette almost as eagerly. Smoking it in nervous, hasty fashion, she said, "You are so kind. I knew it would be all right if I could once get to you."

"Would you like something to eat?"

"No. I don't think I shall ever want to eat again. I'll tell you what happened, then you'll understand. I'm the only one who knows, apart from them — that is why they want to kill me. Linda, they killed him. They shot him dead. And I was there. I still feel sick when I . . ." She looked for a moment as though she might lose the sustaining coffee, but with a shudder forced back the nausea, ground out what remained of her cigarette in the saucer, and immediately reached for another.

"We were in bed," she said. "We didn't share a room except sometimes. . . . They went into his room first, from the terrace, and then came into mine. I wasn't quite asleep. I heard a sort of mutter, not quite a whisper. One of them said, "With *her* there?" And Mr. Lopez said, "Yes, yes. It must be *now*." I switched on my lamp. They had a torch. There were four of them. José half woke up and said, "Can't you sleep?" That was the last thing he ever said. "Can't you sleep?" A soldier got hold of me and one of the others shot José in the chest, through the heart. There wasn't any noise." In her face, always pale, now bleached, and marked where tears had mingled with dust, her eyes gave back a reflection of that terror, that shock.

Linda said, with feeling, "How horrible!"

"And then, for me, it was worse. It was so humiliating. Linda, just as I was, no slippers even, just in my nightdress they took me down, to the barracks beside the palace and put me in a cell, with a guard, a soldier, who could see me all the time and said the most terrible things to me. I shall feel the shame as long as I live." She covered her face with her hands. "I was there for hours, and after such a shock . . ." An ordeal for any woman and for one with Dolores Heredia y Heredia's upbringing, so prudish, so sheltered, just that much worse.

"And then?"

"They changed the guard and the new one was Manuel. He used to work in our stables. He gave me the cape and the boots — all he could find and told me how to get out. There again, Linda, I was so frightened. Anybody might have seen me and what the first guard said showed me how I was *hated* — I'd never guessed. But I came out into that farmland and I only saw one old woman, keeping geese. She never even looked at me. In the jungle I was safe enough. And I knew that if I could get to you, you'd help me."

"I willingly would, Dolores. But what can I *do* ?"

"Hide me."

"But my dear, how could I ? This isn't my house."

"I know. It's Mr. Gordon's. He's English. They are always good to the ill-done-by."

"Mr. Gordon wouldn't shelter you for one moment, Dolores," Linda said brutally.

"Not if *you* asked him, *begged* him ?"

Linda explained Mr. Gordon's pre-occupation with keeping his wife from the slightest anxiety, his aversion to any kind of meddling, his avowed intention of getting along with the government of the day. "He's one of the kindest men on earth," she ended, "but I know, I absolutely know he'd hand you over without the slightest hesitation. He'd hate doing it, but he'd do it."

There was a long pause. Then, almost resignedly, Dolores said, "Well . . . at least you can lend me some clothes, Linda. Whatever happened, I should feel better able to bear it if I were dressed properly."

Was it then, at the moment of saying — but of course, anything, anything — that the idea struck? Vague, unrealistic, perilously near boys'-adventure-storybook stuff. But just possible. *Just*.

Dolores, her story half-told, and the hope that had buoyed her up, quenched, lay on the bed rather as a dead woman might lie. The last anxiety, trivial in comparison with the overall situation — "Let not poor Nellie starve," "Look after my cat," allayed. Whatever happened Dolores Heredia y Heredia could face it better, properly dressed.

"When did all this happen?"

"On Sunday night."

"When did you last eat?"

"That night."

"And this is Wednesday afternoon. Look, I'll bring you some food and some clothes. There is a bathroom through that door. I'd better look . . ." She did so. It was clean. "You can stay here, but you must not make a sound. It would not be safe even to pull the plug. And I will try, I'll do my very best to think of something. But you must eat. . . ."

Making more coffee, scrambling eggs, Linda thought that no sooner had one reason for secretiveness been removed than another had arisen. She brooded over her plan, which demanded not only full cooperation but a willingness to take risk from another person. Had she the right to demand so much? But what less, what else could she devise?

Meanwhile, she must keep her eye on the time. Mrs. Gordon was to be fetched at five.

* * *

"It's a meat loaf," Mrs. Gordon said, referring to a parcel which Sarah was carrying. "Mrs Wilson was so kind and made such elaborate excuses for giving it to her that I hadn't the heart to tell her . . ." She stopped just in time; had been about to say, "that the situation had changed". Only just in time she remembered that she was not supposed to know that any situation had existed. ". . . that we had already catered for supper."

Linda gave her a sidelong glance and thought, so you knew, all along. I wonder how! What self-control.

Sarah carried the meat loaf into the kitchen and there, in the center of the table stood the rum bottle. The criminal always overlooks something. Everything that had been used in the making of Dolores' meal had been washed and put away; but there stood the bottle, screaming for notice. And of course it was noticed.

"Have you taken to secret drinking?" Sarah asked with that mischievousness that just nudged malice.

"No. Why? Oh that! I meant to use it as flavouring for a pudding."

"And did you?" asked Sarah, who was fond of food.

"No. There was so much washing. And anyway I had forgotten the recipe."

"Pity." Putting the meat loaf down beside the bottle, Sarah lifted her head and sniffed. "What can I smell?"

"Coffee. I heated up what was in the percolator. It seemed easier than making tea just for one."

"I can recognize coffee. This is more like scent. Nice."

Linda then remembered having noticed it too, having thought, amid all the tumultuous thoughts that had assailed her as Dolores fell into her arms — how strange that a scent should persist! Dolores, bursting out of the jungle growth had brought with her the perfume of Dolores in her bedroom, Dolores at the hospital. Women who lived luxuriously had soap, bath oil, talcum powder, sachets to lay among their clothes as well as scent, so that their hair, their skin, everything they owned, became impregnated.

"It may be the new detergent," Linda said.

Using one of her grandmother's expressions, Sarah said, "What will they think of next? Shall I set the table?"

"Please. Not for me. I'm going out."

"With the beau?"

"Yes."

The six o'clock news reflected a growing confidence on the part of the new regime; it announced the details of the game of musical chairs which Mr. Gordon had foretold. The mood was laudatory.

"They don't seem to realize," Mr. Gordon said cynically, "that the implication is that they were all totally unfitted for the posts they held before."

You couldn't say to a man, listening to his own radio, in his own house, expressing his own opinion — Be quiet, I want to hear whether there's anything . . .

There was. Madame Fernandez' condition had not improved, was indeed giving rise to concern. It was very doubtful if she would be able to attend the funeral tomorrow.

Doubtful indeed!

13

"OUT there at Caterina," Angus said, "You were reasonably safe, or at least I could only hope so. At least no mobs on the rampage."

"And in Port Philip?"

"A hell of a mess. Far more damage, far more deaths than they admitted. They're still clearing up. The whole thing so carefully planned, so well-timed . . ."

There was something now, without any direct reference or overt act, rearing up between them, some tracts of experience, his and hers, which denied and defied the easygoing, pleasant relationship, established — it seemed long ago now — in the purser's cabin, and since then carefully cherished and kept in good balance.

"You were in Almerina."

"Yes. Somebody from the Min. of Ag. rang me and said there was a case of suspected swine fever there. I began to get my stuff together and then Poppy Sarmiento rang me and when I told her I was just off she said good, Port Philip wouldn't be very healthy for a couple of days, religious processions generally ended in rioting. Then I rang you. . . . There was something about the way she spoke; and once or twice she'd given signs of being in the know about things. I understand why now, of course."

The story, almost unwillingly told, jolted to a halt.

"Why?"

"She belonged to one of those under-cover groups. Communist. Masquerading as a swimming club. Their particular assignation for Monday was to take over the radio tower. That is where Poppy was shot."

"Shot?"

"Yes, I'm telling this badly, aren't I? To tell you the truth I'm a bit upset."

"About Poppy?"

"About the whole thing. You see, the truth is, she never meant anything to me and I certainly never gave her any reason. I was civil when we met, and we often did, at parties and so on. But last night, quite late . . . Linda, this is the most macabre story; if it hadn't happened to me I'd not believe it. I was getting ready for bed and the telephone rang and a woman asked if I'd go to an address on Rope Walk. Eighty-four. A dog — I swear she said a dog — had been hurt and was in great pain. Well, of course, coming up from the harbor I'd seen what had been going on, cars burnt out, windows smashed, and it did strike me as rather touching that in the middle of such an upset — though it was quiet enough then — some woman should bother. So I went. It wasn't a dog; it was Poppy. She'd been shot in the chest, through a lung. Somebody had dragged her as far as that house and done their poor best, plugged the wound. Dirty cloth of course. I said I'd take her to the hospital — the only hope was to get her there right away; and then all the attendant old women, four or five of them, moaned and yelled and said that if she went to the hospital she'd be killed off; she was now a marked woman; the men in the middle had won again; nobody extreme left or extreme right would come out of the hospital alive. You may believe this or not, but Linda, that is what they said and they wouldn't listen to me. I couldn't fight a lot of old women *and* carry Poppy out to my car. If there'd been a telephone I'd have made a grab at it and screamed "Help"; but there wasn't. Whoever called me had gone out to do it. There was this solid phalanx of old women and Poppy, dying on a bed. And the woman who telephoned me said, "Do something. If it was a dog you'd do something." Well, I had a sterilized dressing, I had a pain-killing injection. I thought, just let me get out of here, having done what they seemed to ask — what she seemed to ask — and I'll get an ambulance and I'll go with her to the hospital and stand by and see there's no hanky-panky. It didn't work that way. . . . Linda, while I was substituting a sterilized dressing for that filthy cloth, she said, well, perhaps deathbed speeches shouldn't be repeated. But she said enough to inform me that she had organized me into going to Almerina. . . . And wanted to see me before she . . . And then she did die. Embolism, I suspect. Maybe I should have left the filthy cloth alone. Maybe I should have picked her up as she was. Maybe if I had, the old women would have given way. I just don't know . . . "

"How horrible for you. I am sorry, truly sorry, Angus."

He did not reply immediately. When he spoke again he said, "Well, no amount of breast-beating will do any good now. And afterward one of the women, the most articulate one, said it was a good thing Poppy had died because otherwise she would have gone to jail — probably for life. She also warned me to be careful what I said on the telephone. Mind you, I always have been. Earlier that evening I'd tried to make this sound like a prearranged trip, not as though we were celebrating. Because, if you ask me, the thing isn't settled yet. The fringe groups wasted their force fighting one another. If they ever combined against the center . . . I very much doubt whether Lopez will have the hold on the army that Fernandez had."

"Do you really feel like dining out tonight?"

"Why not? I can't live like a recluse because that poor silly girl . . . And the sight of a few carefree tourists . . . Now that is what I mean by masterly planning. Did you hear how the problem of gaping tourists was overcome? A free trip round the islands, half a day on St. Agnes, on to Belle Isle, eat your head off, drink yourself silly, see the sights, and all for free. I'm told that only two strong characters were able to resist such temptation. They wanted to see the procession. But they were disappointed. Monday's breakfast disagreed with them both! Oh, come on, Linda, that is quite amusing. I'm afraid I've depressed you."

"No. I was sorry, I am sorry; it was a hateful experience for you. But I've got troubles too! Your poor silly girl is at least out of harm's way. My poor silly girl is locked in the maid's room and will be killed unless I can get her out of Santa Maria pretty smartly."

"What girl?"

"The late president's wife, no less."

She told him the whole story and it lasted until they drew up outside the restaurant at North Point.

There were fewer tourists now that the weather was really hot, but the place was busy; and a good many of the customers were going to complain to friends who had recommended the place for its native atmosphere. The brown-skinned beauties were still there, but they carried trays in their hands and were, if anything, over-dressed in the prim black-and-white of Victorian parlormaids. Full, black skirts just short enough to reveal trim ankles, long sleeves, high necks, cuffs and collars and little aprons of *broiderie anglais*, saucy little caps with streamers.

Remembering Mr. Parker's comments on the subject of the North Point waitresses, Linda said, "Planning here, too. This transformation wasn't worked overnight. There's a Puritan streak."

"And you know, it fails in its purpose. I find this far more attractive. Far more seductive. I'm rather against having every-thing laid out on the slab as it were. But that is a digression. We must give our minds to your friend. Had you anything in mind?"

Linda had deliberaetly chosen a table which, besides being fairly isolated in a corner, overlooked the rocky steps by which the tourists came and went, and the place where the motorboats waited, rocking on the water.

She said, "I've thought and thought. I'm

afraid I haven't come up with anything very practical."

If he did not say it, she eventually must; but she hoped he would, one volunteer being worth twenty pressed men.

She ate heartily to encourage him. She told him about the stolen stores and all the mildly comic predicaments that had resulted. "And I'm sure Mrs. Gordon knew all along. Never a sign. If she were a strong woman, she'd be one to conspire with."

Are you one with whom to conspire?

She did not mention the dead dog, nor the mystery of the MacNamaras' disappearance.

Presently he said, "I have the ghost of an idea. I don't know whether you'll think it practical or not, but it's the only thing I can think of. I have the use of this motor launch. Suppose — I'm now trying this out on the dog as it were — tomorrow night, if you could do something to make her look like one of those . . ." he nodded to a table where four female tourists sat. A varied group, really, two young, one middle-aged, one almost old, varying in shape and in coloring and yet all bearing a certain, indefinable stamp. Was it they all looked as though they had come straight from the hairdresser's and donned clothes straight from the cleaner's? Was it the multitudinous bracelets on slim wrists, on plump? Was it, more subtle, the confidence bred of the American dollar, a confidence symbolized by the enormous, formidable handbags full of travelers' checks.

"Then I could take her to St. Agnes. She'd be safe enough there. It's British — in a way."

It was — because to every problem there are many wrong answers and only one right one — precisely what she had thought of herself.

"Would you be willing to do that? Would it be safe to go to St. Agnes in a motor launch?"

"Yes. In calm weather, which this is. Look, they're beginning to move. Just after nine," he said, looking at his watch. "If you can get her here, tomorrow, I'll get her out. I don't go for this mystic stuff and I know damned well that if Poppy had had her way Madame Fernandez would have had her head chopped off by the clumsiest possible axman, but, well, you know, a tooth for a tooth, it cuts both ways. . . . No, God damn it, look . . ."

Linda looked.

On the shore at what was known as Carib Bay the arc lights turned night into day. Here the note was romantic and there was only just enough light to make the descent of the rocky steps undangerous. Electric bulbs were luminous flowers, to left and to right, among the real ones. Now, suddenly, a white, a searching, a cruel light blazed at the foot of the rocky stairway and there were two of the soldier-policemen, demanding, inspecting, what?

The middle-aged woman at the table said in a carrying voice, "My check, please," to one of the Victorian parlor-maids. Then she said, "Maisie, did you bring your passport? We were told and I should have reminded you."

"I did. It's here some place. . . ." The great handbags gaped, the bracelets jangled; the bits of paper and cardboard which now meant so much, were groped for, made ready.

Linda said, bitterly, "Marco Polo went to Cathay!"

"Never mind," he said, "I have another thought. It's a long coast line. Let's go and pick ourselves a landmark."

14

IT stood, a relic of Santa Maria's turbulent past, a solid, squat tower, guarding an easily accessible stretch of shore. Angus was now fully engrossed with his plan. "This will have the advantage that we can start earlier say seven. Can I have your handkerchief? Mine's colored and wouldn't show up so well." He tied the handkerchief to a bush. "That's your landmark from the road, Linda. We'll note whatever is to be noted as we go back, so that you get your bearings in time. Don't stop too near the handkerchief, in case somebody should notice. Drive on, having drawn her attention to it, and let her walk back. Understand, she'll need stout shoes and stockings, the going's a bit rough. To come back to what I said about tourist's getup. Country woman, the older the better, so if walking back a hundred yards she should be seen — it's unlikely, but unlikely things do happen. . . ." They were back in the car and he drove very slowly, peering from side to side. Within two minutes he gave an exclamation of satisfaction.

"Ha! Just the job! Funny how you never notice what you aren't looking for. Did you ever notice this shack?"

In fact she had, only half-consciously, thinking: deserted, and a good thing too, the sort of hovel against which her father inveighed. Thinking: things *have* improved, all those neat new houses at Santa Barbara...

The wreck of the house, palm thatch and corrugated iron and mud, fallen in on itself, stood a little back from the road and in front of it so many feet had trodden, so many fires burned, that even now the space was clear, except for a few of the hardiest weeds.

"You can stop here. You can turn the car here and tell her to walk on until she sees the handkerchief. Got it?"

"Yes. Angus, you're sure you want to do this?"

"No. I don't want to. Rescuing distressed damsels was never one of my Mitty dreams. But I am against whatever would happen to her, through no fault of her own, unless action were taken. And I can see that you have been put into an untenable position. Any risk I take is comparatively small. If you can just manage to get through tomorrow . . ."

"I think I can. I'll get her up early — I shall be down first. I shall give her some food and she'll just have to take to the woods again until it's time to go. We have a new maid coming in tomorrow, so the room must be empty. And — I rather dread Sarah's eye and nose. They don't miss much." With the burden shared and a prospect of relief within less than twenty-four hours, she was able to tell him, light-heartedly, about the overlooked rum bottle and the lingering scent.

And then the blow fell. In front of the Gordon's house there were dark shapes and undimmed headlights; two soldiers at least, not lounging, alert.

"My God! Too late!" Angus said.

She said hastily, "Don't stop; drive straight on. You can drop me and turn round at the end of the road. You mustn't be involved in this."

"I'll drive on, but I won't drop you. You come back to Port Philip and go into hiding.

The very place; that Rope Walk house. They'd never think of looking for you — or for her — *there*. And I'll get you out, somehow."

"I can't! I can't. This will about kill Mrs. Gordon. And it's on account of me. Angus, please, stop. Let me out."

"Your being hauled off to jail won't help Mrs. Gordon." As he spoke he turned at the end of the cul-de-sac.

"Angus, I swear to God, if you take me down to Port Philip I shall simply walk back, or go straight to the police. And I shall never speak to you again as long as I live. I *must* go in — a shock like that . . . How could they explain? Who would believe them? I must . . . I must . . ."

"Then I'll come in with you," he said, drawing up behind the smaller of the two vehicles, a squat jeep. The other was a covered army truck.

"What good will that do. Go along, get away. Please. Please. I don't want you involved."

"I am al . . ." One of the soldiers opened the door on Linda's side.

Going into the house he took her hand. "Don't be too scared," he said. "You're

206

English. And I shall move heaven and earth."

In the living room, coming to it as they did, prepared for the worst — the scene was farcical. Mrs. Gordon reclined in her usual position on the sofa, toying with one of her little drinks. An officer, wearing captain's insignia, sat in an armchair, holding a whisky and soda. Similarly equipped, Mr. Gordon sat in another chair, his expression untroubled and his voice easy and gossipy. Whatever he was saying, he broke off as they entered. He stood up.

"Hullo, my dear. Had a nice dinner? Nice to see you, Angus. This is Captain Sandoval. Mr. Hamilton. Miss Ransom. Something most dramatic has happened and we are being searched."

Captain Sandoval had risen and acknowledged the introduction with a stiff little bow. Seating himself again, he said, "I was particularly anxious to see Miss Ransom." He was not even middle aged but his face was austere, his glance searching and cynical.

"You may," he said, "be able to help us. The situation is this. Madame Fernandez, as you have no doubt heard on the radio, was most profoundly distressed. So much so that the balance of her mind was disturbed. She was given a mild sedative which had the opposite effect. In short, still distressed and also dazed, she wandered out of the palace wearing only her night attire."

Mr. Gordon, without asking their preference, had poured whisky and soda for both Linda and Angus; one weak; one strong. Presenting them, he said, "That's the part I find incredible. A woman off her head and in her nightdress couldn't get far without being noticed."

Ignoring the interruption, Sandoval said, "It is understood that under stress the mind often reverts to childhood. And you were a friend of Madame Fernandez in the early days, were you not, Miss Ransom?"

"We were at school together."

Upstairs, in the bedroom of the master and mistress of the house, heavy footsteps moved. Where did a search begin? Upstairs? Downstairs? Perhaps the last place, when someone was missing from a palace, would be the servants' quarters. Would the back of the house be watched, too?

"Angus, would you mind? I would like

some ice in this. You know your way about our kitchen, don't you?"

"Was the friendship resumed when you returned from England?"

"That was hardly possible, Captain Sandoval, if you think of our relative positions."

"Just so. That is the argument. Quite plainly Madame Fernandez has lost all sense of position and might, it is thought, seek out, seek comfort from old friends."

"A reasonable assumption," Linda said.

"Has she made an appeal to you, Miss Ransom?"

On the frail, the frailest, the most hopeless of hopes that Angus had opened that door and said, "Run!" Linda braced herself and said, "No."

"Then — and this is where you can help. Could you name anyone to whom she is likely to have turned in such a critical moment."

Angus came back with four cubes of ice on a saucer. He said, holding them to Linda, but addressing Mrs. Gordon, "I now understand why all domestic help wants a job in Caterina. Your maid's door was open, Mrs. Gordon, and I took the liberty of peeping in. Positively palatial!"

Please God, let not relief, nor gratitude, nor bewilderment show on my face.

Mrs. Gordon said, "Well, I tarted it up a bit this evening. I like to start off right, however it may end."

"Thank you, Angus," Linda said. "About Dolores' friends, Captain Sandoval. Let me think. It's a long time ago, you know. And to be honest — she was always somebody a bit apart. Very strictly brought up. We were friends in the classroom, but she never came to my home, I never went to hers."

The clumping footsteps were now on the stairs. The living room door opened. A soldier, a sergeant, young but with that same stern, intent look, said, "Sir, nothing anywhere."

Inside Linda's head something exploded, leaving a deafening silence.

Faintly through it came voices, faraway whispers.

False voice saying, "A mere formality, Mr. Gordon. Thank you for your co-operation." Hearty voice, "Well, I knew it was nonsense. Woman in a nightdress, barefoot . . ." Reassuring voice, puzzled but faithful, "Give me a ring in the morning, Linda." And her own, as soon as she could master it. "I have remembered one name, Captain Sandoval, but I am afraid it will not help much. Manda Parsons. Her father was American, rather important. A journalist, I think, making some investigation about wages and living conditions. Dead against what he called the British Raj, if I remember rightly . . ."

"You remember rightly, Miss Ransom. Miss Parsons inherited her father's tendency to be against whatever was. Three years ago she was deported from Santa Maria as an undesirable alien; and is now, I believe, in Madras."

* * *

The jeep, the truck, Angus' car, roared away.

Mr. Gordon said, "Poor Sarah. What with all this, I forgot that she felt sick. Perhaps I should . . ."

"Sarah felt sick," Mrs. Gordon said quite firmly, "because I made her wash up. I did not think that a new woman, coming in, should be faced with a lot of dirty dishes. After all she is now ten and she is going to live in a world where everyone must wash his own dish; she might as well get used to it. And Sarah could always be sick at will."

"I'll look in on her," Linda said. "I have one small job to do first. Good-night."

Taking three of the used glasses, she went into the kitchen. There she switched on the outside light and went, not nervous now, to the end of the line of washing and from there called in a voice as penetrating as she could make it without letting it be noisy, "Dolores! Dolores!" There was no answer and she advanced to the jungle's edge and there called again. She could only think that Dolores had heard the men arrive, or been warned by a hunted creature's instinct, and had slipped away. One particularly sickening thought occurred to her — suppose Dolores had suspected that she had played her false, lulled her with a promise of seeing what could be done, and then betrayed her. In her present state of mind and body it was enough to make her suicidal! Sentiment whimpered, Oh no! Oh no! Common sense suggested that if Dolores had felt suicidal she would not have run; she would have given herself up, with dignity.

She reentered the house at last and went upstairs.

* * *

Sarah had rearranged her bedroom. The bed which usually stood clear was pushed up against one wall in a position that would make bedmaking difficult but left a good deal of space. The huge teddy bear — the only toy Sarah had preserved from earlier years — sprawled across the foot of the bed, toward the wall; beside him there was a book. Sarah was sitting up in bed with her knees hunched high, and between her knees and her chest was an ordinary chamber pot. Her face was flushed, her eyes, with widened pupils, looked dark. Linda knew a swift pang of compunction. Poor little girl, truly sick for once, doting father otherwise engaged, doting mother remembering false cries of wolf in the past. Driven to seek solace from the bear which usually sat on the chest of drawers.

Before Linda could say a word of sympathy or inquiry, Sarah said, "Go down and tell them I'm quite all right and sound asleep."

"I'm not sure that you are. You're quite

213

flushed. I think I'd better take your . . ."

"Please Linda! This is no time for argument. Do as I say. Then come back here, but through the bathroom." They shared a bathroom, both bedrooms opening into it.

"Have you actually been sick, Sarah?"

"I soon shall be. If you don't go and head them off I shall be so sick. . . . Don't you think they've had enough for one evening? Linda, please. *I've* had enough for one evening, let me tell you. . . ."

She sounded slightly delirious. Soothe, pacify.

"All right. I shan't be a minute," Linda said. She ran down and gave the message. Mr. Gordon said, "Good!" Mrs. Gordon said, "What did I tell you?" They all bade one another good-night again.

Now Sarah sat on the side of the bed. The sheet and the light gay cotton cover, all that were needed at this season in the way of bedclothes, were rolled back. Close to the wall, occupying no more than a third of the bed, Dolores lay in a sleep so closely resembling death that for a second, until she saw the rib cage lift and fall, Linda was frightened. She said, "You . . . you . . ."

"I'm flushed," Sarah said ironically. "Who wouldn't be?"

"How did you? What led you?" Linda stammered.

"I was being helpful. I went to take in the things you'd washed. As I put the outside light on, I saw, at least I thought . . . I thought I saw a ghost in Theresa's room. Pale, and it moved. I was scared to death. I thought it was one of Theresa's zombies. And then I remembered my grandmother. . . . She believed in them, not zombies, plain ghosts, and she said they were very lonely and unhappy and you should *speak* to them, kindly. Gosh, I nearly made a muck of the whole thing. I was so scared, really. I put the light on. If Daddy had come into the kitchen just at that minute . . . But he didn't. And she told me and I could see . . . That wasn't a safe place at all. So I brought her up here and I gave her one of Mummy's pills. She's rather like the Sleeping Beauty don't you . . . Linda, give me that bowl. Quick."

She pulled up the cover, hunched her knees. And just in time. The sergeant had come back. An old, a well-tried trick. Give a suspected place fifteen minutes, then go back and nine out of ten times you found what you were looking for. You can come out now! Weren't we clever? Didn't we fool them properly?

In fact this man, a kind, loving father, was relieved to see that the poor little sick girl was having some attention. On his first round he had thought, not for the first time, that English people were peculiar, always on about stray dogs and overloaded donkeys and then, when it came to their own flesh and blood, so hardhearted.

Well, in this case the old trick had failed and he remembered the other half of his errand. Because Linda was holding and steadying the sick child, he addressed her with more than his usual civility. "I am sorry, Miss Ransom, I have to request your passport. All Santa Marian passports are subject to check."

Precisely what Helen had said. Feeling almost as sick as Sarah quite definitely was being, Linda went to her room, found her passport and handed it over. Now I am trapped, too.

"It will be returned to you in a few days," the sergeant said.

"My grandmother," Sarah said, looking down at Dolores, "would say it was the hand of God. She got out of prison, she found her way here, she found you alone — Daddy would have shooed her off, wouldn't he? Then I found her, just in time. I saved her really. And we're lucky not having a maid; making my own bed, doing my own room tomorrow morning. But what about the day after?" She answered herself. "Oh, I shall say I don't want a new woman in my room until we know she's honest."

"I very much hope she'll be gone by tomorrow evening," Linda said and gave a brief outline of the plan.

"That's the kind of beau to have," Sarah said approvingly. "We're going to have a bit of trouble making her look like an old country woman. . . ." She scowled in concentration. "Mummy did have some stuff that made you look suntanned, but it didn't suit her much so she may have flung it away. Brown shoe polish? I'll think of something."

The thing which had so often peeped out and mocked and then vanished so quickly that looking at the beautiful, candid, blue eyes you wondered if your sight had tricked you, or your imagination was doing overtime, was there now. But it seemed fully disposed to be helpful. And it was an indisputable fact that, but for Sarah, Dolores would now be on her way back to Port Philip. One could have a worse ally.

"I'm afraid, Sarah," she said, apologetically, "you won't sleep very well on that little bit of the bed."

"I am going to sleep on the floor. Did you know, that used to be a form of penance in religious houses, in the Middle Ages. No bed for a week, Brother Ambrose!"

*   *   *

In her ordinary, comfortable bed, Linda slept badly, slept hardly at all, approaching again and again that narrow verge on sleep's border where fact and fantasy were indistinguishable, and then jerking back from some horror. In the morning, gritty-eyed and with a head stuffed with sawdust, she went along softly to Sarah's door in the landing; it was locked. So was Sarah's door to the bathroom. Linda went down to get breakfast, thinking — here again lucky in that I control the food. In ordinary circumstances this could have been far more difficult.

Sarah came down; fresh as paint in a T-shirt that matched her eyes and white shorts.

"I don't think that pill I gave her suited her, Linda. Mummy takes two every night; I only gave her one, but she's very dopey. And shivery; hot and cold at the same time, if you know what I mean?"

Not knowing, but able to make some guesses. Delayed shock? The effect of a sleeping pill prescribed for another person? Malaria? An infected scratch or thorn prick on a body so carefully protected that it had developed no immunity?

All she could say, since life must go on, apparently untroubled, was, "Try a cup of coffee, Sarah. Then you must come down to breakfast in the ordinary way. I must be there, too. I'll go up as soon as I can. Don't worry, darling, please."

15

"I... NEVER... did... anybody... any... harm," Dolores said, in the voice that Sarah called dopey but was, Linda knew, the voice of delirium. Linda squinted at the thermometer — one hundred and three. No wonder Dolores sounded woolly. God, not malaria, it takes days and days and she must be on her way this evening.

Downstairs, Tessa had arrived accompanied by Miguel and his bicycle, so loaded with bundles and baskets and parcels that it would have been impossible for him to ride it. So he pushed it.

Upstairs, Mrs. Gordon lay in her bed. "I think I'll take a little rest, Linda. Last night was a bit of a strain. I couldn't help thinking how dreadful for her and how dreadful for us, had she, as they seemed to think, have come here. I know I'm a weak sister, a bent reed. But I think I'll stay in bed for a bit. I'll be up for lunch."

And here, in this secret room, watched

by the child who should now have been engaged in arithmetic, Linda shook down the thermometer, and after asking questions to which she received vague and often contradictory answers, given in the faraway voice of fever, found what she thought was the cause of the trouble, a nasty looking, suppurating sore where the army boot had blistered one heel, and then rubbed the blister away and gone on chafing the raw flesh beneath. Upward from it, over the swollen ankle radiated the ominous, red streaks of blood poisoning.

"It must be very painful."

"It *was*. Better now." And that was ominous, too.

Hot *salt* water had been one of the remedies which Doctor Ransom had advocated, perhaps because in the poorest hovel water could be heated and salt produced. But there were swifter cures nowadays and leaving Sarah, mouse-quiet between the two locked doors, to apply this immediate first aid, Linda braced herself to face the MacNamara's empty house. There she knew that in the little room, the counterpart of Mr. Gordon's study, Doctor MacNamara kept certain supplies.

In his person, in his ordinary habits Doctor MacNamara was one of the untidiest men alive. "Where it falls it lies, so far as he is concerned," his wife said. He always looked as though he had dressed in a hurry in the dark, and a newspaper after he had given it one casual glance was calamitously crumpled and disordered; but his little room was meticulously neat. It was not a dispensary in the ordinary sense of the word; down in Santa Barbara there was now a chemist's shop. Nor was it a surgery; down in Santa Barbara there was a place called the clinic. It was a little room, lined with shelves, glass-fronted, as nearly dust-proof as possible. There was a table, a chair, a filing cabinet, a shelf full of medical books, a pile of journals.

In such a place, had I been a worthy daughter of my father, of my mother, I should feel completely at home; as it is, all that I know is that I need penicillin and that penicillin can be administered by pill — slow; by injection — quick. This must be quick; Dolores must be reasonably fit by seven o'clock this evening. And well before that she must understand what she is supposed to do, and to be. I have never administered an injection in my life; hypodermic syringes fill me with an unreasonable horror. Even in the dentist's chair, the aim a painless filling, "It sounds silly. I can't bear the sight . . ." "That is not at all uncommon," the dentist said. "During the war I had to give injections to men who were going abroad. About five percent, yes, quite that, fainted."

Little glass capsules, little bombs with necks ready to be broken off. Presumably one shot. One shot how often? Who is to answer that? "Disposable; use once and discard," said the label on the case of syringes. Take three, or four. Did anyone ever die from an overdose of penicillin? Was it something to which people could be allergic? But what else can I do but try? I have done my best. But wasn't that always the cry of those who failed?

* * *

"You could fool me," Sarah said, stepping back and surveying her own handiwork with an artist's satisfaction.

The injection, clumsily and painfully administered by an unpracticed and amateur hand had worked the modern miracle. By two o'clock Dolores' temperature was normal; the red lines receding not encroaching, her mind capable of understanding what was required of her, what had been done for her.

"The gratitude I feel cannot be expressed in words," she said. It might, if she got away, if this scheme worked, be expressed in another way Her father had shot himself, but her mother and three old aunts had survived and had been allowed to go to Miami. Fernandez simply had not wanted them around, dour and black-clad and disapproving. They had taken with them enormous wealth, not only in money, but in goods — two Goya portraits of the young Heredia y Heredia who had been in Madrid in 1775 when the painter was living hand-to-mouth, glad of any patron . . . things like that. And most of all the jewels with which the men of the family had bedecked their wives over four centuries. If she got away, got to America, Linda and Sarah and this man, Angus, would be very much rewarded, rich past anything they had dreamed of. . . . But she was not sure that even if all went well, she'd ever get to Miami. She felt very queer.

Sarah said, "Nails, we nearly overlooked them." She clipped them very short and not very evenly, and then rubbed into what was left of them, and around the cuticles a stick of charcoal from her drawing equipment. Then, with an artist's gesture and an artist's pride she surveyed the finished work. Two hidden cardigans and two hidden petticoats lent bulk, and the visible clothes combined to a nicety the two conflicting trends which governed the apparel of women of the type Dolores was supposed to be — the Spanish preference for black, so dignified, so utilitarian; the Caribbean weakness for primary colors. Every member of the household had contributed something, wittingly or unwittingly; over hair deliberately roughened and lopsidedly pinned up, Dolores wore one of Mr. Gordon's yellow and scarlet bandanas; her black skirt, its hem made uneven and the whole of it soiled, had been part of Mrs. Gordon's smartest suit; it gaped at the waist over the extra clothes and was secured by a large safety pin; the blue blouse was Linda's; the tennis shoes, Sarah's, the only footwear in the house which could be trusted to stay on and not to put pressure on the injured heel. Even the bandage, inexpertly wound and soiled on the outside was in absolute keeping. A poor old country woman, or rather a poor woman, prematurely aged by poverty, a bit ailing, a bit lame.

"In a long journey in an open boat at night," Linda said, "she might feel cold."

"She can have Teddy's rug," Sarah said, making the supreme sacrifice. Her grandmother had taught her to knit, and in order to evoke some show of enthusiasm, had suggested making a rug for Teddy; and so that the child should not become bored, she had provided wool in many colors, to be knitted into squares and then feather-stitched together. Two birds with one stone! "They do carry things like that, tied up by the corners," Sarah remarked.

As they worked Linda and Sarah had spoken mainly to one another because for Dolores it seemed to be a great effort to speak and sometimes took a long time to answer even when directly addressed. Yet her temperature was now normal and the improvement in the festering heel almost incredible.

"How do you feel now, Dolores?"

"All right. Just queer. Not like myself."

"You don't look like yourself, either," Sarah said with a cackle of laughter. "It is a pity you can't go along and look in Mummy's long glass." The imp danced. "Dare we risk it?"

"No. Getting out will be risk enough."

"It'll be all right. They're having their little drinks and I shall go down and say something that will start an argument while you slip out."

Linda did not ask *how*. There were ninety-nine ways of starting arguments and Sarah knew them all.

Sarah went first. On the unlighted stairs Linda stood, with Dolores close behind her. She heard the argument start, a muddle of voices, no words.

"Now," Linda said and they slipped out of the house.

What Sarah had said was, "Daddy can I have a pink gin?"

"No, you most certainly cannot. What put that into your head?"

"Something I read in an advertizement for Angostura bitters. It was invented around here to stop Nelson's sailors getting ill."

Mrs. Gordon said, "How interesting. I never knew that."

"Well, can I then, Daddy?"

"I have said no once. Nobody should touch spirits under the age of twenty-one."

"But you can't drink Angostura bitters on its own. I shall catch Yellow Jack and die."

It went on; Mr. Gordon prepared to compromise, just a teaspoonful, a dash of bitters and a lot of cold water. Mrs. Gordon compromised — if after this one taste Sarah would promise not to touch spirits again until she was twenty-one, she would give her her pearls, Ten years from now! The pearls would be Sarah's long before that. Sarah, having heard the Seagull move away, compromised. Could she try the bitters in the sweet vermouth. Why not; with happiness so threatened, why not be happy now?

16

AT the crossroads Linda turned on to the road toward North Point. "Sleep if you can," she said.

"I am, almost. Asleep," Dolores said in the way which Sarah had so aptly described as dopey. Was it reaction from strain? A sleeping pill hangover — if so, surely extremely prolonged. An overlarge shot of penicillin? You could worry yourself to death, thinking one minute that the morning's dose had been too large, and at the next that it would perhaps have been wise to give another.

The she saw that she had something else to worry about. Ahead, separated by the width of the road, two red lights, stationary; and between them, waving from side to side a white one, very bright.

"There is a roadblock," she said. "Don't say anything until I have explained."

She slowed and halted.

The man with the extremely powerful torch directed it at the Seagull's number plate and then at the paper he held in his other hand. He was not alone. Two more of his kind — soldiers? policemen? — stood by the red lights.

"Mrs. Gordon?"

"No. I am the Gordons' governess and I am taking our new help to pick up her belongings."

The merciless light shone upon Linda's face. I hope I don't look anxious, it is an innocent errand; and upon Dolores. Would the disguise stand up.

"So now I am to be blinded, being lame already. Son of a mule!"

Whose voice? The voice of the island; of one who used English when it must, a debased form of Spanish at home. It was querulous in tone, in intent abusive. It was the voice of the grandmother of the man with the lantern and he reacted automatically, redirecting the beam to the space between the two bucket seats; nothing there; to the back of the car, empty. Addressing, not Linda, but the old woman he said, "I must examine the boot." And he did so. There was nothing there. Before he waved them on he made the proper reply to the one who had called him son of a mule, but he made it in Spanish and was answered in that tongue — not in the Spanish of the Heredia y Heredia family, in phrases picked up, collected, like stamps or butterflies, from Manuel, the stable boy.

*　*　*

"You were marvelous, Dolores."

"I was afraid. . . . If he had asked us . . . to get out. To be drunk and fall down is not permitted. As I am now, to scold is permitted. And I am tired of it all."

Still slightly off key. And into the darkness the headlights tunneled, wave after wave of blackness breasted and thrown back. Presently the ruined hut where she must stop, send Dolores on her way to look for the handkerchief that blazed the trail.

All day, because Dolores had seemed so vague and because she was hoping for some improvement, some alertness, some positive collaboration, Linda had avoided going into details about this final stage of the operation. Now she tried.

"Dolores, I must stop here because it is a place where I can turn. You walk along and you will see a handkerchief on a bush and there you go down to the beach, toward the old tower. Mr. Hamilton will be there. We are exactly on time. He will take you to St. Agnes."

"You have been so kind. Everybody has been most extremely kind," Dolores said. She fumbled ineffectually with the handle of the car door. She had probably never in her life opened or shut one for herself. Linda hurried round, opened the door and more or less pulled her out.

"Handkerchief," Dolores said, leaning on Linda, "which way?"

"Are you all right?"

"Yes. Not quite myself. You have been so kind, Linda. Did you say on a bush?"

"Yes, lean on me. This way."

"The only thing to do," Dolores said, "when people are rude is to be rude first."

She walked with a bit of a limp, but that was to be expected; what disturbed Linda more was a curious lack of direction or purpose about her movements. Uncoordinated, like her talk.

They reached the bush which Angus had marked and Dolores said, reasonably, "You were right. I thought I must be mistaken. A handkerchief on a bush."

"Yes, we turn off here and go down to the beach."

"It is rather late for that. But everybody has been most kind."

Linda removed the handkerchief marker, horribly aware as she did so of the far more obvious and glaring giveaway in the shape of the car, just along the road.

Last night the plan had been for her to deposit Dolores, turn around and go home. They had not considered roadblocks, simply the idea of an English car drawing as little attention to itself, and to the place of escape as was possible. The roadblock had altered that and between it and the ruined hovel she had worked out her plan. Not to go straight back; drive on to North Point, park, somewhere out of sight. Wait ten minutes — long enough for the new help to discover that someone in her family was ill, or to decide that she did not, after all wish to work in Caterina.

One thing had conflicted with another. The best laid plans . . .

"It is very uneven," Dolores said.

"Not very far now." It was rather like humoring and cajoling an intoxicated person. Once, so long ago that it could not be counted in any measure of normal time, she and Charles had been out. He drove a red sports car, was teaching her to drive, but on that evening, when the fog closed down, sudden and blinding, he was driving and she said, "Darling, please, go a bit slower, we can't see." And he said, "If there's anything to see, you see it." And there was some truth in that. There was the tower, visible, a darker thing in the darkness, and there between the darkness of the land and the darkness of the sea was the shifting line of foam which each wave gave up, expired upon; a dying note.

"Here we are," Linda said. She flicked her lighter and looked at her watch. "Dead on time."

Seven o'clock, zero hour. If there's anything to see, you see it, even in a blinding fog. The veterinary launch would be a blur against this smooth, favorable sea; a blur, a blob, taking on shape and substance.

At the foot of the old tower the sand, pinkish, very fine, retained some of the day's heat.

"How do you feel, Dolores?"

"Better, sitting down. I was so afraid to be asked to stand. I never could you know;

even Fernandez understood that. It was a joke; everytime I stand up I fall down. Twenty minutes in an hour, on the hour, however formal."

Half-past seven, a quarter to eight; ten to, five to, Eight. Where are you? What has happened to you? What has gone wrong? And what is going wrong behind me? If they patrol the road; that known, that so-recognizable car.

If there's anything to see, you will see it. And there, on what seemed to be the edge of this calm, lisping sea, went the motorboats, gaily lit, carrying the early tourists back from North Point to Port Philip. Half-past eight. A qurter of nine, and presently nine.

Two hours late. And that meant that he would not come now. Could not come. Blank failure, and below the failure a creeping sense of unease. I was obviously suspected; he was seen with me; by association he may be suspected, too.

And here she was on this desolate beach with a woman ailing in body and not quite right in mind. Throughout the long vigil, Dolores had not proffered a single remark or question about the situation in which she found herself. Once she said, "They chose Miami because it is warm," and once she repeated her comment about everyone being so very kind. Asked how she felt now she said, "All right, but rather queer."

It seemed senseless to wait any longer. Linda helped Dolores to her feet and with her arm around her waist, hauled her over the sand through the scrub and on to the road. The approach to the waiting car was nerve-racking. The derelict hut could be an ambush. In her mind Linda prepared an explanation, so frail as to be absurd — the poor woman, unused to this mode of transport had been terribly carsick, so they had gone into the bushes. Why, they would ask, on that side of the road; what is wrong with the bushes on this side.

But nobody stirred. She then remembered, almost too late, that she had overlooked a vital thing. At the roadblock she had said that they were fetching the new help's belongings. There must be a bundle. This involved undressing Dolores and removing her extra clothing. Not enough. Women of that kind tended to own valueless things in bulk. The glove compartment yielded a head scarf that belonged to Mrs. Gordon, a box that had contained a hundred cigarettes and now held five, a paperback book and a lump of pink stone which Sarah had picked up on the beach and retained because water erosion had affected it freakishly and it bore a definite resemblance to a human head. To this collection Linda added her own single undergarment and her sandals. Tied in Teddy's rug and placed on the car's back seat, it looked likely enough. Pray God they wouldn't search it; and there was no reason why they should — it was a woman they were hunting, not some piece of lost property.

"I think, Dolores, you had better pretend to be asleep this time; let your head sag. That might account for your looking smaller now. Do you understand me?"

"Oh yes. That will be easy. One of the easiest things I was ever told to do," Dolores said, rather touchingly.

"A ticklish job," people said when a job demanded tact or special skill. Driving a car barefoot was a veritably ticklish job, the sole of the foot tended to recoil automatically from the touch of the accelerator or brake, and the toes seemed to regain, after uncounted centuries of loss, some of their old prehensibility.

It was the same man; he made the same search.

"She has gone to sleep," Linda said. "It has been a long day for her." He had no desire to wake the old scold. He waved the car on.

"Dolores, there is now the business of getting you back into the house. You must wait in the car, in the garage until I am sure the coast is clear. Do you understand that?"

"You sound," Dolores said, "exactly like Mother Marie Joseph. She always said I was stupid. But I understand."

"How do you feel now?"

"All right. I should be better if things wouldn't keep moving about."

"We shall soon be home and I'll get you to bed as soon as I possibly can."

* * *

Mr. Gordon said genially, "You know very well, Linda, that you don't have to account to me for your movements; but you ought to give your beau a clue. He rang up the moment you left and twice since. He

sounded quite agitated the last time —
about ten minutes ago. You'd better
talk to him. I'm off to bed. Good-night."
He added, as he went to the door, "You
missed a damned good dinner. I thought
Theresa could cook, but this new one has
the pants off her."

"Angus, it's Linda."

"Hullo, Linda. This a very *bad* line.
Can you hear me?"

"Can you hear *me*?"

"Well enough; but it *is* a bad line."

She knew what that meant.

"So long as we can just hear."

"I wanted to apologise for this evening.
I had transport trouble."

"I see. I did wonder. All right then,
you're forgiven. Transport trouble no
man can be blamed for."

"I always said you were a girl in a
million. But now, wait for it. Missing
today, late tomorrow. Could you make it
eight? It's all a bit of a muddle you see.
The veterinary launch is out of commission,
but I have to go to Almerina — these
pigs, you know. But a very kind policeman
is going to take me over in a police launch."

"And bring you back. In time for our date."

239

"That rather depends. It is just possible that I may have to come back alone. It's a bit hard to explain on this crackling line. Can you still hear me?"

"I can hear you."

"The point is, I'm the veterinary. I can advise and exhort but I don't carry the ultimate authority. Over this swine fever job authority is the only answer and it could be necessary to leave the policeman to exercise it on Almerina. In which case I shall be out on my own with a very new, very powerful police launch, very different from my old scow. But I rather look forward to it. And to our date. Eight o'clock then? All right?"

"Don't take any risks with it."

"Crackling and buzzing," he said, "it's like talking to a bee hive. Did you say risk? Don't be silly. Anybody who can kick my old tub into action can have himself a ball with a police launch. Eight o'clock then tomorrow. Till then . . ."

"Good-night, Angus. As they say, if you can't be good, be careful."

"Good-night, Linda. Pleasant dreams."

There was so much in that cautious, listened-in-to, "this is a *bad* line" conversation that needed to be thought over; but no time now. She put down the telephone and went, softly upstairs and tried Sarah's door. Back in full possession of her bed, Sarah was reading — of all things, *Rebecca of Sunnybrook Farm.*

"I was waiting to hear," Sarah said. "All right?"

"All wrong. Sarah, I'm sorry; something went wrong. We have to wait, to hide her for another twenty-four hours. Something happened."

"The beau chickened out?" Sarah came back from a vanished world where a girl of her age could say of a sunshade, "It's the dearest thing in the world, but it's an awful care," and prepared to deal with realities. To spend another night on the disciplinary floor.

Linda stole down, brought Dolores in and up, walking the knife edge; one clumsy footfall . . . And as she pushed her into Sarah's bedroom the door bell rang.

Tracked, hounded down, spied upon. Watched by the derelict hut, followed home. Going to open the door to the inevitable she framed sentences in her mind — nobody else was concerned; I take the entire responsibility.

And, opening the door, she saw that the worst had happened.

"Colonel de Saucedo," he said, khaki-clad, black-buttoned, brisk, upright, in any other context very good looking, but now the concentration of menace. "Miss Ransom?"

"Yes. Come in." Nobody else is concerned; I take the entire responsibility. Sad about Dolores, sad about me, but it has always been like this, innocent or at least semi-innocent people caught up in movements that they did not visualize, understand or do anything to bring about.

From the head of the stairs a far from genial voice said, "And what now? Look here, young man, I've had about enough of this." Mr. Gordon in his pajamas. "What do you want?"

"Mr. Gordon, I am sorry to have disturbed you. Colonel de Saucedo. I have to ask a few questions of Miss Ransom. It will not take long."

"She answered questions last night," Mr. Gordon said, belligerently. "We all answered questions. The house was searched from top to bottom. Then, just as my wife was falling asleep you coming ringing that infernal bell."

The young man said again, "I am sorry. I have orders. A few further questions to ask of Miss Ransom. Would you prefer that I questioned her elsewhere?"

"No, I would *not!* Last night I let that lot go through my house without a search warrant. But I'm not allowing anybody to be taken out of my house, so don't think it."

"I should myself prefer to ask the questions here, sir."

"I'll get my dressing gown."

"It is essential that I see Miss Ransom in private."

"It's all right, Mr. Gordon. I don't mind," Linda said. She could hear her own voice, breathless, nervous, guilty. The front of her dress shook to the rhythm of her hurrying heart.

"It will not take long," Colonel de Saucedo said again.

He followed her into the sitting room and took the chair she indicated. She was glad to sit down.

"Miss Ransom, I am conversant with the answers which you gave to Captain Sandoval last evening. In effect, you were a friend of Madame Fernandez when you were at school together, but had not, since your return, resumed what might be called friendly relations."

"That is what I said. Yes."

"In January," he said, quite casually, "at the president's reception, she *made* an opportunity to have a private talk with you. It lasted twenty minutes."

Who had watched, and seen, despite all Dolores' precautions, and reported?

"Yes."

"In February there was a little ceremony at the hospital — arranged for you, as your father's daughter. Madame Fernandez canceled a far more important engagement in order to be present. She again spoke to you, informally."

"That is true."

"Yet you deny that she was your friend?"

"In the sense that you mean, yes." Voice steadier now. They *suspected*; they still did not *know*.

He said, "The outcasts have no

244

friends. All over Santa Maria, the cock crows very loudly just now, Miss Ransom."

Linda thought, psychological warfare! Sent to provoke me, to make me say — of course we were friends. But she did not say it. They were not sure yet, still probing. Fend them off; less than twenty-four hours now to go — if Angus could find some way of ditching the very kind policeman. And how?

She said, "It may seem so, Colonel de Saucedo. Is that all you wished to ask me?"

"No." He said the word slowly and then sat silent, staring at her more searchingly than even Captain Sandoval had done. Then he said, "It is a risk I must take." He unfastened the top two buttons of his tunic and from an inner pocket brought out a buff envelope, sealed. A thickish package. "If you already know where she is, or if she should come to you, give her this, please." He held the envelope out across the table between them. Linda made no move to take it.

That was the worst of suspicion, it corrupted everything; and she was capable of thinking two things so close together that they seemed simultaneous. She thought — another secret friend! And she thought — very clever indeed!

"What makes you think that I could deliver it?"

"I was not sure, Miss Ransom, until I spoke of the cock crowing. Then your eyes denied the accusation of disloyalty. For less than a second; but they denied it."

That was quite clever too. He pushed the package toward her and then, as she made no move to take it, dropped it on the table.

"It is of the utmost importance. Truly a matter of life and death."

He stood up and rebuttoned his tunic.

Linda said, "What you choose to leave in this house, Colonel de Saucedo, is entirely your own affair. I wish now that I had a witness to the fact that I have not touched that package or undertaken to deliver it."

"Before a witness I should not have produced it. And if my reason and my instinct are both at fault and you pick up that telephone and report me you will be told that there is no Colonel de Saucedo on the army list. I wish you good-evening, Miss Ransom; and if I am right about you, I pray God keep you."

Both the doors to Sarah's room were locked and a gentle scratching on the one in the bathroom received no answer. The package spent the night on Linda's dressing table and once again she slept badly.

17

"IT could be a booby trap," Sarah said. "I've read about such things; watches that blow up when you wind them. I'd be very careful about opening it. In fact I'm not sure I'd open it at all."

"What was he like, Linda," Dolores asked, weighing the package in her hand.

"Good looking. I'd say pure Spaniard. Nothing remarkable. In fact, it shot through my mind when he said that he had not used his own name — suppose he were genuine and I betrayed him, could I pick him out in an identification parade. I decided I couldn't."

"And there was no message at all ?"

"No."

"They certainly want me dead — but not blown up in the house of an Englishman," Dolores said. "I was to end through suicide, from grief."

She broke the seal, opened the envelope and spilled out on to the bed several documents, the most immediately recognizable an American passport made out in the name of Mrs. Maisie Pennington of Davies, California. Except that Mrs. Pennington wore her hair in an almost shoulder-length bob, parted at the side, the likeness between her and Dolores was uncanny, the same fine dark eyes, the same delicate features. She was obviously a woman of some substance, fond of travel, able to indulge her whims and perhaps for that reason, a little indecisive. She had entered Santa Maria a week ago and if it suited her could embark this very afternoon, Friday, on the English S.S. *Avon* making its way to Jamaica; or if she cared to wait four days, she was free to join the French *Ronsard*, which would take her to Nassau, and points beyond. And if she found Santa Maria so fascinating that she wished to stay another four days, the *New Orleans* would take her direct to the city after which it was named. Indecisive woman, she had marked them all on brochures, on maps, on sailing time-tables; extravagant woman, she had bought tickets as though they were luncheon vouchers. And every one in order; stamps applied where stamping was necessary, bits torn off exactly where they should be torn. If in a world ruled by regulations, by bits of paper, any woman could be said to be foot-free, Mrs. Maisie Pennington was that woman. She had American Express checks for ten thousand dollars.

"Only one person in the world could have or would have done this for me," Dolores said. She was better this morning; the sore on her heel was drying up, closing in on itself, the muzziness of her mind cleared.

And it was just half-past eight. Still time to save Angus from taking whatever action he proposed to take.

She rang and his woman answered. "Mr. Hamilton has gone. Try laboratory."

"Mr. Hamilton has left for Almerina. Just now. Can I help you?" It was the voice of the one willing-to-learn, anxious-to-try student?"

"Could you catch him?"

"I am afraid not. Today he was obliged to go to Almerina in a police launch. He was running. But if there is anything I can do . . ."

"Thank you. No, nothing."

So many nasty, nasty little lies.

"Mrs. Gordon, Sarah says her tooth aches. I think I should run her down to Port Philip.

"Oh, poor darling," Mrs. Gordon said. "If you wouldn't mind, Linda, I should be eternally grateful to you. I once had," she said, hooking and zipping her skirt, "an experience — traumatic, you could call it — with Sarah and a dentist." The skirt adjusted, Mrs. Gordon sat down, a little hurriedly, on the stool before her dressing table. God, I look ghastly; and rouge no longer serves. Do what I may, it looks like a clown's paint. "I had to take her to the dentist's. It was a baby tooth, it could have been pulled out, but he said preserve them as long as possible because they kept the way open, made way for the permanent ones. So he said he would fill it. You know what that means? Drilling. Linda, I sat there, I held her hand — she held mine, so hard that I couldn't use it for a couple of days. And I thought — this is what is so shocking — that if I truly loved her I would have wished myself in that chair, under the drill. But, do you know, I did not. I simply could not. I knew then . . . Who said that courage was the one virtue that made the others possible ?"

"I can't place it, Mrs. Gordon. But there are many sorts of courage. A lot of people who would — and could — face a dentist's drill, lack the other sort."

"Oh, that old bromide! Moral courage ? Putting a brave face on, making the best of things. But, Linda, ninety percent of people do that every day. No virtue there."

"I think you are extremely brave." There was a second's mutual embarrassment. "Well, if you would take her, I shall be very grateful."

Mrs. Gordon picked up the charm bracelet which she wore every day though she would have preferred not to; its jingling often irritated her; but Mr. Gordon had given it to her soon after their marriage; it had then held a single trinket, a small gold heart. Since then he had sought and found small golden objects representative of every country they had lived in together, or that he had visited alone, of any outstanding occasion, anniversaries, birthdays. He liked her to wear it, so she wore it. And now, rising from her stool she went to the window, the better to see to adjust the catch, and looked out and said, "Linda. Look!" This bedroom window overlooked the space in front of the houses and outside the MacNamara's stood Doctor Mac-Namara's battleship-grey Toledo.

"They're back! Oh, I have been so *worried*," Mrs. Gordon said, admitting the truth at last. She began to run.

"You must not run," Linda said, running herself and catching Mrs. Gordon at the head of the stairs, breathless already.

"Take it easy. Hang on to me, I'll come across with you."

There was time; the *Avon* sailed at four o'clock; boarding began at two-thirty, and in the bedroom Sarah was already working out what Mrs. Maisie Pennington was likely to wear, likely to carry, and mourning over those closely cut nails.

*   *   *

"I was just coming to you," Ian said. "Is Rufus with you? Is he?"

"Why, no dear," Mrs. Gordon said, stopping in her greeting to Ian's parents. "We haven't seen him, have we?"

"I did, Ian," Linda said quickly. "I knew he'd wandered off, so I was looking out for him. Actually I'd brought him some supper. . . ." How freely the lies ran. "But he didn't want it and he seemed very tired, so I let him in, to his own bed. And in the morning, when I looked in . . . Ian, I'm sorry, but he had died in his sleep. I spoke to my friend — you know — Mr. Hamilton, the veterinary, and he said that was the very nicest way for an old dog to go. Just to go to sleep, in his own bed and not wake up."

The boy's gray eyes filled with tears and he bit his lower lip. "That's all right then. Thank you, Miss Ransom. Thank you very much. I was just afraid . . . well you know . . . either tied to a stump and starved, or running wild and being stoned . . . But he was old. I always knew I'd outlive him. Thank you for putting him to bed . . . for the . . . last . . . time . . ."

That was too much; he swung away to cry without being observed.

And how many faces, how many changing expressions could one observe at one moment. Mrs. Gordon shot Linda a look curiously like one of Sarah's, blue and penetrating; the parents gave her a less subtle look — a good lie, but thank you for it. Why did they think she lied? Because this was a time for lies and they were themselves if not actually lying, evasive.

"I was so concerned for *you*," Mrs. Gordon said. "Even when I'd made George ring the hospital and they said you'd gone fishing, I was not quite easy in my mind."

"Fishing was, roughly, the idea," Doctor MacNamara said, "but it didn't work out. Not that I could know . . ."

"It isn't often that I lose my head," Mrs. MacNamara said, avoiding Linda's eye, "but when I do, I do a thorough job. The way I went into the hospital, in my apron, screaming for Hamish and Ian, the wonder is that we didn't all . . ."

"We were given protective custody," Doctor MacNamara said, avoiding everybody's eye.

"In the palace," Mrs. MacNamara said. "Quite luxurious. Now how about a cup of coffee? I'll make it myself, I think. That poor girl has enough to do, the way I left the kitchen and she all worn out from nursing and burying her aunt."

Linda said she must not stop for

coffee, she had to take Sarah to the dentist. Doctor MacNamara said he had patients to see. But as soon as he and Mrs. Gordon were alone for a moment he turned to her and asked,

"Are you all right. I hope nothing happened to upset *you*."

"Only a searth party on Wednesday evening. They seemed to think that we might be harboring Madame Fernandez — because of Linda, you know; they were at school together, long ago. They little know George!"

"He would have turned her away?"

"It sounds heartless — but what else could he have done?"

"True enough. It's none of our business."

What else could *I* have done? Doctor MacNamara asked himself. The man was dead, had been dead for hours when I saw him. No amount of inquiry into how and why and when would have brought him back to life. Port Philip was not an English coroner's court where careful investigation might serve the cause of justice. And to have refused to act with *Them* would have brought instant reprisal, perhaps even death, not only to himself, but to Janet and Ian as well. He was thankful that Madame Fernandez' disappearance had spared him a repetition of unethical conduct. . . .

Starting up his car and setting off on his round, he made up his mind to take advantage of being in favor with the new regime and ask permission for Ian to go to school in England.

* * *

"You still don't look *quite* right," Sarah said, regarding Dolores, now disguised as Mrs. Maisie Pennington. "Apart from the nails, I mean. I know! A camera! They always have cameras. It'll have to be Daddy's, I'm afraid, mine isn't expensive enough."

Linda's best uncreasable cotton dress — nylon too hot for this time of year; Mrs. Gordon's sun hat, a native product of fine white straw trimmed with raffia flowers; Sarah's white sling-back sandals; Mrs. Gordon's best handbag crammed with everything that an American lady tourist would carry for a day's outing, all her papers, her money, cigarettes and lighter, cosmetics, sun glasses, a bulging packet of

Kleenex. Mr. Gordon's camera, a Leica, completed the outfit.

"Now!" Linda said, having spied out the land, "quick!"

They hurried down and huddled into the car, Dolores sitting low between them.

"At the first hint of a roadblock, I shall get out, throw up the bonnet and tinker. Under cover of that you get out and walk. Or sit down by the side of the road and try to get another lift. Even in that guise you must not be seen with me. I'm already suspected."

"I understand," Dolores said. "My thanks to you I can never express; there are things too deep to put into words."

"I've enjoyed every minute of it," Sarah said.

Dolores' mind, conventional and old-fashioned, had already apportioned tokens of the gratitude she felt. Sarah must have the family sapphires, Linda a dowry; and both must come to Santa Maria by round-about means, ostensibly from Sarah's god-mother in Paris whose address Dolores had scribbled down on a scrap of paper.

Linda hoped that the roadblock would not be encountered too soon; Dolores' heel was better, but the wound was still open, and in order to wear the sandals she had been obliged to dispense with all dressings, save some strips of plaster.

Sarah was to act as lookout and, anxious as she was to have the nerve-tearing trip over, Linda drove rather slowly so as to be able to stop quickly. She did so when just outside the town, Sarah hissed, "Stop." Linda got out on her side, leaving the door wide, Sarah did the same on hers. Linda threw open the Seagull's bonnet which yawned like a crocodile. Sarah stood by her door, widening the amount of cover behind which Dolores could leave the car and reach the verge of the road. There was no time for leave taking. Linda fiddled about inside the car, slammed down the bonnet and drove on. Dolores sat down in the nearest patch of shade and with shaking fingers lighted a cigarette.

At the roadblock Sarah, her hand to her cheek, explained their errand. "I have toothache; I have to go to the dentist."

The soldier, having looked into the back and boot of the car said, standing back, "If your car is troublesome there is a garage that I can recommend. It is opposite the hospital. Very reliable and cheap." It was kept by his brother-in-law. Families should stick together.

"And now, I suppose," Sarah said when they had been waved on, "I *must* really go to the dentist, in case we are tailed."

"I suppose so. Yes. But honey, you haven't really got a toothache, so there'll be nothing to be done."

"I wouldn't be too sure," Sarah said with dismal cynicism. "I may be like that boy who cried wolf once too often."

* * *

This time it was Linda's hands that she gripped and crunched as the drill whirred in what the dentist called "a cavity of some size". Considerably shaken, very pale and somehow reduced in size, she emerged from the ordeal and said, "I know it didn't actually hurt my mouth, after the first stab, but it hurt *me*, in my mind. People just don't understand about . . . well, imagination. And you know, Linda, if I didn't have, well, whatever it is that makes you feel what you aren't actually feeling . . . is there a word for it ? I mean if that night I'd gone running and saying there was a woman in Theresa's bed. Just think what would have happened. And when that man came to hunt in my room."

It was all strictly true and strictly logical and Sarah was right in needing another word than imagination. Who was it who defined intelligence as an awareness of circumstance? That, more than anything else was what Sarah had, in abundance. The ragged nails for a working woman, the camera for the American tourist . . .

"You have behaved marvelously, Sarah. What would you like to do now?"

"Have lunch at that cafe. One side of my mouth is quite numb, but the other is all right."

Halfway through the meal Sarah said, "There is another thing I want to do," and Linda saw the imp come up and take possession, mischievous, masterful. "I want to see the end of it. And there would be no harm in that. Dozens of people go to watch or to buy things in those tourist traps. I want to see her safe aboard."

"Sarah, I don't think it would do for us to be noticed."

"I am not suggesting that we lean on the barrier and throw kisses. I simply want to go and buy some souvenirs; and the kiosks on the piers are the best, everybody knows."

"Well," Linda said, remembering what an excellent ally the child had been, "so long as we are not conspicuous."

"There'll probably be a crowd. You aren't eating very heartily, Linda. Don't you like what you chose? Have something else."

"I'm still a trifle worried."

"About *her?*" Sarah asked in a lower voice.

"No; though I admit I shall be glad when four o'clock comes. I'm a bit concerned about Angus."

"Gracious! I'd forgotten all about him. Of course he was going . . . But why worried? You can go and tell him it's off. Can't you?"

"Of course. It's the thought of what he may have done before then. To get rid of the policeman and get away with that launch."

"He wouldn't do anything silly, you may depend on that. Far too much like Daddy."

"Look at the silly things you and I have done lately."

"That is true," Sarah said reflectively. "I think I won't bother about that Knicker-bocker Glory. We shall just be in time, if we walk down. My face is coming back to life."

"Outside the cafe she took Linda's arm and gave a hop in order to fall into step. "Try not to worry," she said, "I'm racking my brain to think of something."

18

THIS end of the harbor, which was the first, and last, glimpse of Santa Maria that visitors saw, was very different from the purely commercial end. The hotel stood at the highest point to the right, shining white as a wedding cake, and its gardens dropped, terrace by terrace, almost to water level. Tables with umbrellas, striped red and white, dotted the terraces. Then there were the steps leading down to the little jetty and the place where the motorboats rocked gently on the blue water. The gateway at the top of the steps was closed by a heavy chain, and the motorboat harbor was completely deserted save for a man sitting on the top step. Perhaps to offer some excuse for the inactivity; perhaps to note anyone who seemed anxious to hire a boat. Then, partly on land and partly jutting out over the water were the piers, four of them, even their utilitarian purpose as far as possible disguised by flowering creepers and shrubs and tubs of flowers.

The road here, between the harbor and the town's edge, was wide and on its landward side occupied almost entirely by little cafes, some with gay awnings, some with umbrella'd tables, and flowers everywhere. It would be quite possible, more than possible, almost inevitable that people visiting should go home with the image of an island paradise firmly imprinted on their minds.

And can I blame them, Linda asked herself, making for the arched, flowered entry to Pier 4; didn't I always feel exiled and homesick? Eager to return.

Some of the innocents who would go home and say — such a pretty place; you really should go; let me show you my photographs — were already in the wide space all set about with kiosks offering fruit and flowers, picture postcards and transparencies, dolls in "national" dress — a garb never seen on the island but pretty enough, a myriad little articles made from turtle shell, cans of fish from the installation at Carib Bay.

Laden with gifts for the unfortunates who had not enjoyed this holiday, laden with souvenirs which on some dull winter day would call up memories, they moved in a thin stream, which grew as it approached the barrier, where on either side of the opening a soldier stood. Very pleasant and polite, willing even to hold a bunch of flowers while its owner burrowed into her handbag and produced her passport.

Sarah said, "I want something absolutely hideous for my grandmother in Scotland. It is a joke between us. When I was about four I bought her something in Naples that I thought simply beautiful. She pretended to like it. So I've sent her something as ugly as possible from wherever I have been." She paused and then said, thoughtfully, "But not from here, yet. I must be getting rather old for this game. Maybe I'll send something pretty this time. If I can find anything." Before turning to the displays she said, "Let me know."

Time passed. The stream of would-be embarkers thickened. Either by accident or good judgment, Dolores appeared in the center of a large crowd; and either by accident or design she had found a companion, a man of middle age, obviously American.

Linda took Sarah by the elbow and said, "Haven't you found anything yet?" Sarah turned and said, "Which do you think?" Over the objects which Sarah held they watched the slow shuffle toward the barrier.

Then Linda's heart and breathing stopped. From somewhere where he had been lurking, Colonel de Saucedo emerged and took his place beside one of the soldiers. What a trick! What a trap! Her heart moved again, but so bumpily and so high in her throat that to breathe demanded a definite effort of will. Sarah, who had never seen the arch-traitor, watched unperturbed. Nothing could save Dolores now; but perhaps the child might be spared the sight of so much strain and cunning being brought to nothing.

"Help me out," she said urgently. "I'm ill."

"Gosh!" Sarah said, seeing in Linda's stricken face, paper white and wet with sweat, evidence of this statement. She dropped whatever she was holding and with astonishing wiry strength took Linda by the waist and held her, at the same time saying to the woman at kiosk, "Chair!

Chair! There, sit down. Put your head on your knees."

"Don't look, Sarah. Don't look."

Sarah took that as indication that Linda was about to be sick.

With her face in her lap Linda waited helplessly. I failed, deceived by some sweet talk. I failed even to get Sarah away.

When she ordered Linda to put her head down Sarah had put a hand on her shoulder, and kept it there. Now her fingers tightened and she gave a little grunt of satisfaction, a sound very different from the one Linda awaited. Then she asked, with the greatest solicitude, "Better now?"

Linda raised her head.

Colonel de Saucedo stood exactly where he had been when she last looked. Dolores was a third of the way up the gangway and there she turned and lifted one hand in a curious gesture, not a wave, almost a benediction. There was nothing to indicate to whom it had been directed, nothing to indicate by whom it had been received. The young soldier stood straight and still. The American put his hand under Dolores' elbow to assist her up the gangway's slight incline.

"You missed the great moment," Sarah said softly. "She must have guessed we were here. She waved to us."

One day, when I feel a bit stronger, I will tell you how romantically that story ended, Linda thought, remembering Dolores' words about knowing what love was.

"And now, I suppose," Sarah said, "having flung these beautiful things on the floor *and* borrowed a chair, I must spend lavishly."

She did so, and in return the woman who sold the souvenirs offered a piece of advice.

"Did the lady eat something disagreeable to her? It is necessary to be careful where one eats. The Cafe Granada is the cleanest and safest place in all Santa Maria."

It was kept by her cousin and his wife. Families should stick together.

"Where is it?" Sarah asked.

"Just across the road, almost immediately opposite."

Idly, almost in that mood of detachment which accompanies convalescence after severe illness, Linda heard this conversation and at the same time watched what was going on halfway between where she sat and Sarah stood. The floor was made of heavy planks, treated with concrete, and dusty. Just above one of the joints in the flooring a scrap of paper lay, a scrap about the size of a quarter of a postage stamp. It was suddenly lifted and twisted on what looked like a corkscrew of brown dust which held it suspended, four inches above the floor's surface, and then let it go. In Santa Maria, at this season, she remembered, a sure sign of bad weather. "When the Dust Devil dances, take shelter," was an island saying.

Getting up from the chair she said, "Sarah, I think we should get home."

"When you are fit to drive. You need a cup of tea. And the world owes me a Knickerbocker Glory. We'll try this Granada place."

Outside, though the sun no longer shone it was hot, the world was hushed away, smothered under a great heavy eiderdown, the sky, colored purple, lowering, threatening.

"Well, we did it," Sarah said. "And how very dull life will be, from this time forth and forever more. Like Napoleon on St. Helena. But at least we've had it, haven't we? A bit of excitement. Something a bit different..."

Spoon poised over her Knickerbocker Glory, Sarah plainly regretted that the period of stress and strain was over and done with. Linda, a cup of tea before her, thought of Angus who might have devised some risky, reckless way of getting rid of a policeman and obtaining possession of a police launch — all to no purpose now. And a storm coming up.

Sarah ate two luscious spoonfuls and halted the third. "I can see it," she said. "It says 'Harbor Police', I wonder ... I have been racking my brain. Nowadays even Laplanders herding reindeer have walkie-talkie sets. Wouldn't you think that perhaps even here..."

"It's worth trying," Linda said and was up, out of the cafe across the road before Sarah had emptied the spoon.

* * *

The office was a bleak room, smelling strongly of disinfectant. Only one man was on duty behind the long counter and although his "Yes, madam?" was civil enough his glance was quelling.

"It's about . . . about a police launch," Linda said, and the sergeant allowed himself a look of surprise. He had taken her for a tourist — and they were without discrimination and believed that a place plainly labeled harbor police was suitable for the reporting of lost property. "It left for Almerina this morning, taking Mr. Hamilton, the veterinary. . . ."

"That is so," the sergeant admitted, but not until he had consulted one of the papers before him.

"I wondered whether . . . I mean are the launches equipped . . . Could you communicate with it ?"

"Naturally. How else could we operate ?"

"Then would you *please* send a message to him, to Mr. Hamilton for me ?"

"I regret," he said with pleasure, "that that is quite impossible. Police radio is not for public use."

"I know. I know. But I thought that for once . . . as a favor. It is rather important."

"I regret."

"Is there anyone . . . Can I speak to whoever is in charge here ?"

"I am in charge here, at present. But the inspector himself could not vary the rules."

She tried to steady herself with the assurance that Angus would do nothing foolish, nothing too obviously risky; and yet one never knew. And in the present state of affairs anything even a little different could be dangerous. She had a crazy feeling that unless she got out of here promptly she might be arrested for making a disturbance in a police station. That ludicrous thought triggered off something that should have been amusement but turned out to be tears. To hide from this hard-faced fellow the fact that she was crying she swung round sharply and there was Sarah.

"Didn't it work? Oh what a shame. Poor Miss Ransom!"

More often than not she used Linda's Christian name now, reserving the surname for moments of mockery or resentment or formality. It rang out now because to see Linda crying marked an occasion. "Come on," she said, "let's go home."

"One moment please," the man said. "Miss Ransom . . ." It was now his turn to speak jerkily, unconfidently. "Is it that you . . . Are you related to the late Doctor Ransom?"

"His daughter," Sarah said savagely. "He worked himself to death here and everyone remembers him with *gratitude* — till she asks for a tiny . . ."

"Please, Sarah . . ."

"I am one who has reason to remember," the sergeant said. And out of the hard shell of officialdom and fear of putting a foot wrong, the human being shot a cautious head. "But rules," he said and withdrew; only to emerge again. "Wait please . . ." the human being said, and went to the end of the counter where there was a telephone with a whole bank of keys in its base. He pressed one. He said to the quacking gabble that resulted, "So? So! Forestalled by two minutes, eh? Ah, but I have a nose for weather." He replaced the telephone and looked up, smiling. "We are fortunate. A weather warning. What would you wish to add to the message about to go out to PL Isa 2, Miss Ransom?"

"Please say — *Everything rearranged. Not tonight. Tomorrow at Caterina.* Is that too long a message?"

"Once contact is made for an approved reason the length of the message is immaterial. You would wish to add?"

"Yes, two words. *Love, Linda.* Thank you so very much."

He scribbled the message on his pad. He would relay it, of course, having said he would, and having admitted that he owed a debt of gratitude to a man, now dead, who had saved his mother's life. Nevertheless he scowled at the message, so trivial, so silly. A lovers' tryst which something had prevented and *she* had thought it worthwhile to ask assistance from the harbor police in order to make her fatuous rearrangements. What was the world coming to, he asked himself, and like others before him who had asked that question, he received no answer.

THE END

FICTION TITLES IN THE ULVERSCROFT LARGE PRINT SERIES

OCTAVO SIZE

Wyatt's Hurricane	*Desmond Bagley*
Landslide	*Desmond Bagley*
Letter from Peking	*Pearl S. Buck*
The New Year	*Pearl S. Buck*
The Melting Man	*Victor Canning*
The Long Corridor	*Catherine Cookson*
The Unbaited Trap	*Catherine Cookson*
Hannah Massey	*Catherine Cookson*
Love and Mary Ann	*Catherine Cookson*
A Song of Sixpence	*A. J. Cronin*
A Pocketful of Rye	*A. J. Cronin*
Shannon's Way	*A. J. Cronin*
Flowers on the Grass	*Monica Dickens*
Magnificent Obsession	*Lloyd C. Douglas*
My Friend My Father	*Jane Duncan*
The African Queen	*C. S. Forester*
Hornblower in the West Indies	
	C. S. Forester
The Ship	*C. S. Forester*
Flying Colours	*C. S. Forester*
For Kicks	*Dick Francis*

Flowers for Mrs. Harris and
Mrs. Harris goes to New York
Paul Gallico
Sandals for my Feet   *Phyllis Hastings*
Beauvallet   *Georgette Heyer*
The Convenient Marriage
Georgette Heyer
Faro's Daughter   *Georgette Heyer*
Devil's Cub   *Georgette Heyer*
The Corinthian   *Georgette Heyer*
The Toll-Gate   *Georgette Heyer*
Bride of Pendorric   *Victoria Holt*
Mistress of Mellyn   *Victoria Holt*
Menfreya   *Victoria Holt*
King of the Castle   *Victoria Holt*
Kirkland Revels   *Victoria Holt*
The Shivering Sands   *Victoria Holt*
Atlantic Fury   *Hammond Innes*
The Land God gave to Cain
Hammond Innes
Levkas Man   *Hammond Innes*
The Strode Venturer   *Hammond Innes*
The Wreck of the Mary Deare
Hammond Innes
The Lonely Skier   *Hammond Innes*
The River of Diamonds   *Geoffrey Jenkins*
The Safe Bridge   *Frances Parkinson Keyes*
The Brittle Glass   *Norah Lofts*

OTHER FICTION TITLES IN THE ORIGINAL ULVERSCROFT LARGE PRINT SERIES

QUARTO SIZE

A Breath of French Air	*H. E. Bates*
The Darling Buds of May	*H. E. Bates*
The Fabulous Mrs V.	*H. E. Bates*
All the Days of Minnie-Sue	*Susan Bell*
That Summer's Earthquake	
	Margot Bennett
The Manasco Road	*Victor Canning*
Grand Canary	*A. J. Cronin*
A Bit of a Bounder	*Mary Ann Gibbs*
The Healing Touch	*Philip Gibbs*
The Captain's Table	*Richard Gordon*
Lost Horizon	*James Hilton*
The Wrong Side of the Sky	*Gavin Lyall*
At the Villa Rose	*A. E. W. Mason*
November Reef	*Robin Maugham*
Jamaica Inn, Vol. 1	*Daphne du Maurier*
Jamaica Inn, Vol. 2	*Daphne du Maurier*
The Man from Martinique	
	Shirley Murrell
House-Bound	*Winifred Peck*
Lonely Road	*Nevil Shute*
A Sunset Touch	*Howard Spring*

NON-FICTION TITLES IN THE ULVERSCROFT LARGE PRINT SERIES

OCTAVO SIZE

OTHER NON-FICTION TITLES IN THE ORIGINAL ULVERSCROFT LARGE PRINT SERIES

QUARTO SIZE

These Ruins Are Inhabited *Muriel Beadle*
The Hills Is Lonely *Lillian Beckwith*
I Walked Alone *The Earl of Cardigan*
Living Dangerously
F. Spencer Chapman, D.S.O.
The Gardens of Camelot
Rupert Croft-Cooke
Finn the Wolfhound *A. J. Dawson*
One Pair of Hands *Monica Dickens*
I Bought a Star *Thomas Firbank*
Come Hither, Nurse *Jane Grant*
Return to the Islands *Arthur Grimble*
New Zealand Journey *Jeanne Heal*
The Kon-Tiki Expedition *Thor Heyerdahl*
The Why of Albert Schweitzer
J. Franklin Montague
This Time Next Week *Leslie Thomas*
A Fly in Amber *Susan Wood*